BROTHER BERSERKER

Also by Fred Saberhagen

BERSERKER'S PLANET

Fred Saberhagen

Brother
Berserker

Futura Publications Limited
An Orbit Book

An Orbit Book

First published in Great Britain in 1969
by Macdonald & Co. (Publishers) Ltd.
Orbit edition published in 1975
by Futura Publications Limited,
49 Poland Street, London W1A 2LG
Copyright © Fred Saberhagen 1969

ISBN 0 8600 78264
Printed in Great Britain by
C. Nicholls & Company Ltd.
The Philips Park Press
Manchester.

Futura Publications Limited
49 Poland Street,
LONDON W1A 2LG

PART ONE

Lieutenant Derron Odegard leaned back in his contour chair for just long enough to wipe his somewhat sweaty palms on the legs of his easy-fitting duty uniform, and to minutely shift the position of the padded headset on his skull. He performed these nervous actions without taking his eyes from the tangled green pattern on the wide, slightly curved viewscreen before him; and then he leaned forward again and resumed his hunt for the enemy.

After only half an hour on watch he was already bone-tired, feeling the weight of every one of his planet's forty million surviving inhabitants resting crushingly on the back of his neck. He didn't want to bear the burden of responsibility for any of those lives, but at the moment there was nowhere to set them down. Being an officer and a sentry gained a man a bit of material comfort, and a bit less regimentation when he went off duty—but let a sentry make one gross mistake on the job and the entire surviving population of the planet Sirgol could be tumbled into nothingness, knocked out of real-time and killed—more than killed, ended so completely that they would never have existed at all.

Derron's hands rested easily and lightly on the moulded controls of his console; there was a good deal of skill, though nothing like love, in the touch. Before him on the screen the green tangled cathode-traces shifted at his will, like tall grass put aside by the hands of a cautious hunter. Thus symbolic grass through which he searched represented the interwoven lifelines of all the animals and plants which flourished, or had flourished, over a certain few square miles of Sirgol's land surface, during a few decades of time, some twenty thousand years deep in the prehistoric past.

Surrounding Derron Odegard's chair and console were those

7

of other sentries, a thousand units all aligned in long, subtly curving rows. Their arrangement pleased and rested the momentarily lifted eye, then led the eye back to the viewscreen where it belonged. The same effect of encouragement to concentration resulted from the gentle modulations that sometimes passed like drifting clouds across the artificial light which flowed from the strongly vaulted ceiling of this buried chamber; and from the insistent psych-music that came murmuring in and out of headsets, airy melodies now and then supported on an elemental, heavy beat. In this chamber buried below many miles of rock, the air was fresh with drifting breezes, scented convincingly with the tang of the sea, or with green fields, at different times with all the varieties of living soil and water that the berserkers' bombardment had wiped away, months ago, from Sirgol's surface.

Again, the traces representing interconnected life rippled on Derron's viewscreen at his touch on the controls. In the remote past, the infra-electronic spy devices connected to his screen were moving at his command. They did not stir the branches nor startle the fauna in the ancient forests they surveyed. Instead they hovered non-interferingly just outside reality, avoiding most of the nets of paradox which reality spread for man or machine that travelled in time. The spy-devices lurked just around the local-curves of probability from real-time, able to sense even from there the lines of powerful organization of matter that were life.

Derron knew that his assigned sector, nearly twenty thousand years back, was somewhere near the time of the First Men's coming to Sirgol, but he had not yet seen the trace, unmistakably powerful, of a human lifeline there. He was not looking for humans especially. What mattered was that neither he nor any other sentry had yet observed the splash of disruptive change that would mean a berserker attack: the gigantic machines besieging the planet in present-time had perhaps not yet discovered that it was possible here to invade the past.

Like a good sentry in any army, Derron avoided predictability in his own moves as he walked his post. From his seat in remote physical comfort and relative physical safety he monitored the signals of one spy-device after another, ranging now a decade further into the past, then five miles north; next two years up-time, then a dozen miles southwest. Still no alien predator's passage showed in the lush symbolic grass that grew on Derron's screen. The enemy he sought had no lifelines of its own, and would be visible only by the death and disruption that it broadcast.

"Nothing yet," said Derron curtly, without turning, when he felt his supervisor's presence at his elbow. The supervisor, a captain, remained looking on for a moment and then without comment walked quietly on down the narrow aisle. Still without lifting his eyes from his screen, Derron frowned. It irritated him to realize that he had forgotten the captain's name. Well, this was only the captain's second day on the job, and the captain, or Derron, or both of them, might be transferred to some other duty tomorrow. The Time Operations Section of Sirgol's Planetary Defence Forces was organizationally fluid, to put it mildly. Only a few months ago had the defenders realized that the siege might be extended into time-warfare. This sentry room, and the rest of Time Operations, had been really functional for only about a month, and had yet to handle a real fight. Luckily, the techniques of time-warfare were almost certainly entirely new to the enemy also; nowhere else but around the planet Sirgol was time travel known to be possible.

Before Derron Odegard had managed to recall his captain's name, the first battle fought by Time Operations began. For Derron it began very simply and undramatically, with the calm voice of one of the communications girls flowing into his earphones to announce that the berserker space fleet had launched toward the planet several devices which did not behave like ordinary missiles. As these weapons fell toward the planet's surface they vanished from direct observation; the sentry-screens soon discovered them in probability-space, falling into the planet's past.

There were five or six objects—the number was soon confirmed as six—dropping eight thousand years down, ten thousand, twelve. The sentries watching over the affected sectors were alerted one after another. But the enemy seemed to understand that his passage was being closely followed. Only when the six devices had passed the twenty-one thousand year level, when their depth in the abyss of time had made observation from the present practically impossible, did they stop. Somewhere.

9

"Attention, all sentries," said a familiar, drawling male voice in Derron's headset. "This is the Time Operations Commander, to let you all know as much as I do about what's going on. Looks like they're setting up a staging area for themselves down there, about minus twenty-one thousand. They can shoot stuff up-time at us from there, and we probably won't be able to spot it until it breaks into real-time on us, and maybe not until it starts killing."

The psych-music came back. A few minutes passed before the calm voice of a communications girl spoke to Derron individually, relaying orders for him to shift his pattern of search, telling him in which dimensions and by how much to change his sector. The sentries would be shifting all along the line, which meant that an enemy penetration into real-time was suspected. Observers would be concentrating near the area of the invasion while still maintaining a certain amount of coverage everywhere else. The first enemy attack might be only a diversion.

These days, when an enemy missile dug near the shelters, Derron rarely bothered to take cover, never felt anything worse than the remotest and vaguest sort of fear; it was the same for him now, knowing that battle was joined, or about to be. His eye and hand remained as steady as if he knew this was only one more routine training exercise. There were advantages in not caring very much whether death came now or later.

Still he could not escape the hateful weight of responsibility, and the minutes of the watch dragged more slowly now than ever. Twice more the imperturbable girl-voice changed Derron's search sector. Then the Time Ops Commander came back to officially confirm that an attack was on.

"Now keep your eyes open, boys," said the drawling voice to all the sentries, "and find me that keyhole."

At some time deeper than twenty thousand years in the past, at some place as yet undetermined, the keyhole must exist—an opening from probability-space into real-time, created by the invasion of the six berserker devices.

Had men's eyes been able to watch their arrival directly, they would have seen the killing machines, looking like six stub-winged aircraft, materialize apparently from nowhere in a spot high in Sirgol's atmosphere. From the compact formation in which they had appeared, the machines exploded at once like precision flyers, to scatter in six separate directions at multisonic speed.

And as they separated, the six immediately began seeding the helpless world below them with poison. Radioactives, antibiotic chemicals—it was hard to tell from a distance of twenty thousand years just what they were using. Like the other sentries, Derron Odegard saw the attack only by its effects. He perceived it as a diminution in the probability of existence of all the life in his sector, a rising tide of morbidity beginning in one corner of that sector and washing slowly over the rest.

The six machines were poisoning the whole planet. If the First Men were on the surface at the time of this attack, it would of course kill them; if they landed later they would wander baby-helpless to their deaths in a foodless, sterile world. And with that, the descendants in present-time of the First Men, the entire surviving population, would cease to exist. The planet and the system would be the berserkers' for the taking.

The rising odds on world-death spread up through prehistory and history. In each living cell on the planet, the dark tide of non-existence rose, a malignant change visible on every sentry-screen.

The many observed vectors of that change were plotted by men and computers working together in Time Operations' nerve centre. They had a wealth of data to work with; perhaps no more than twenty minutes of present-time had passed from the start of the attack until the computers announced that the keyhole of the six enemy flying machines had been pinpointed.

In the deeper catacomb called Operations Stage Two, the defensive missiles waited in stacks, their blunt simple shapes surrounded by complexities of control and launching mechanism. At the command of Operations' computers and their human overseers, steel arms extended a missile sideways from its rack while on the dark stone floor beneath it there appeared a silvery circle, shimmering like a pool of troubled liquid.

The arms released the missile, and in the first instant of falling it disappeared. While one set of forces propelled it into the past, another sent it as a probability-wave up through the miles of rock, to the surface of the planet and beyond, into the stratosphere, straight for the keyhole where the six devices of the enemy had entered real-time.

Derron saw the ominous changes that had been creeping across his screen begin suddenly to reverse themselves. It looked like a trick, like a film run backward, like some stunt without relevance to the real world.

"Right in the keyhole!" yelped the Time Ops Commander's voice, drawling no longer. The six berserker devices now shared their point of entry into real-time with an atomic explosion, neatly tailored to fit.

As every screen showed the waves of death receding, jubilation spread in murmurous waves of its own, up and down the long curved ranks of sentry posts. But caution and discipline combined to keep the rejoicing muted. The remainder of the six-hour shift passed in the manner of a training exercise, in which all the i's were properly dotted and the t's crossed, the tactical success made certain by observations and tests. But beneath the discipline and caution the jubilation quietly persisted. Men who were relieved on schedule for their breaks passed one another smiling and winking. Derron smiled like everyone else when someone met his eye. To go along, to show the expected reaction, was socially the easiest course. And he did feel a certain pride in having done a good job.

When the shift ended without any further sign of enemy action, it was certain that the berserkers' first venture into time-warfare had been beaten back into non-existence.

But the damned machines would come back, as they always did, thought Derron. Stiff and sweaty and mentally tired, not bothering to smile any more, he rose from his chair with a sigh of relief to make room for the sentry on the next shift.

"I guess you people did all right today," said the replacement, a touch of envy in his voice.

Derron managed one more smile. "You can have the next chance for glory." He pressed his thumbprint in the appropriate place on the console's scanner as the other man did the same. Then, officially relieved, he walked at a dragging pace out of the sentry room, joining the stream of other members of his shift. Here and there another face stayed as grim and tired as he knew his own must look. But once they had passed through the doors which marked the area of enforced quiet, most of the men formed excited groups and started to whoop it up a little.

Derron stood in line to turn in his recording cartridge with its record of his shift activity. Then he stood briefly in line again, to make a short oral report to one of the de-briefing officers. And after that he was free. As if, he thought, freedom had any meaning these days for a citizen of Sirgol.

A huge passenger elevator, one of a string that worked like buckets on an endless belt, lifted him amid a crowd of others out of the deeper caves of Operations to the housing level of the buried world-city, where there were still miles of rock overhead.

The ideal physical environment of the sentry room was not to be found on Housing Level or anywhere else where maximum human efficiency was not considered essential at all times. On most of Housing Level the air tended to be stale at best, and at worst burdened with unpleasant odours. The lighting along most of the grey street-corridors was no better than it had to be. In most public places decoration was limited to the ubiquitous signs and posters, which in the name of the government exhorted the people to greater efforts for victory, or promised them that improvements in living conditions were on the way. Here and there, such improvements were slowly being made. Month after month, the air became a little fresher, the food a little more varied and tastier. Given the practically limitless power of hydrogen fusion to labour for them upon the mineral wealth of the surrounding rock, it seemed that the besieged planet-garrison might sustain themselves indefinitely, in gradually increasing comfort.

The corridor in which Derron now walked was one of the main thoroughfares of the buried world-city. His bachelor-officer's cubicle was one of the housing units which, mixed with shops and offices, lined its sides. The corridor was two stories high and as wide as an ordinary main street in some ordinary minor city of the late lamented surface-world. Down its centre were laid moving belts, ridden in either direction by people who had to go farther than they could conveniently walk. Derron could see pairs of white-uniformed police rushing past on the belts now, checking the dog-tags of travellers. Planetary Command was evidently cracking down on work-evaders.

As usual, the broad statwalks on either side of the moving strips were moderately crowded with an assortment of people. Men and women in work-uniforms monotonously alike were

13

going to their jobs or leaving them, at a pace neither hurried nor slow. Only a group of children just set free from some schoolroom were displaying any excess of energy. A minority of adults and young people, off-duty, strolled the walks or stood in line before the stores and places of amusement. Those places still under some semblance of private management seemed on the average to do a better business than those wholly operated by the government.

One of the shorter queues of customers was that before the local branch of the Homestead Office. Like the other small offices and shops, this was an area partitioned off by wire and glass at the side of the wide corridor. Standing before the Homestead Office on the statwalk, Derron looked in at the lethargic clerks, at the display of curling posters and somehow shabby models. The displays depicted, in colours meant to glow impressively, a number of plans for the postwar rehabilitation of the planet's surface.

APPLY *NOW* FOR THE LAND *YOU* WANT!

Of land there was no shortage. Substances breathable and drinkable, however, might be hard to find. But the Homestead assumption was that sometime—after victory, of course—there would be a good new life for all on the surface, a new life nourished and protected by the new oceans of air and water which were to be somehow squeezed from the planet's deep rock or if need be brought in from the giant outer planets of the Sirgol system.

Judged by their uniform insignia, the people standing in the short line before the Homestead Office were of all classifications and ranks. But at the moment they were all displaying what an earlier age might have called a peasant patience. With eyes that hoped and wanted to believe, they fed themselves on the models and the posters. Derron had stopped on the statwalk mainly to look at these people standing in line. They had all of them somehow managed to forget, if indeed they had ever allowed themselves to grasp the fact, that the world was dead. The real world, the one that mattered, had been killed and cremated, along with nine out of ten of the people who had made it live.

Not that the nine out of ten, the statistics, really mattered to

14

Derron. Or, he thought, to anyone else. It was always only the individual who mattered. . . .

A familiar face, a beloved face, came into Derron's thoughts, and he pushed it wearily away, and turned from the believers who were waiting in line for a chance to strengthen their belief.

He began to walk toward his cubicle once more; but when he came to a place where the corridor branched, he turned on impulse to follow the narrow side passage. It was like an alley, dark and with few doors or windows; but a hundred paces ahead it ended in an arch that framed the living green of real treetops. At this time of day there would not be many people in the park.

He had not taken many steps down the side corridor before he felt the tremor of an explosion come racing through the living rock surrounding him. Ahead, he saw two small red birds streak in alarm across the greenery of the trees. He kept on walking without hesitating or breaking stride, and had taken three more paces before the sound came, dull and muffled but heavy. It must have been a small missile penetration, fairly close by. From the besieging fleet in space the enemy threw down probability-waves that sometimes got through the defences and the miles of shielding rock and then turned into missiles and so into explosions in the vicinity of the buried shelters.

Unhurriedly, Derron continued walking to the end of the passage. There he halted, leaning with both hands on a protective railing of natural logs while he looked out over the dozen acres of park from a little balcony two levels above the grass. From the dome of "sky" six levels higher yet, an artificial sun shone down almost convincingly on grass and trees and shrubbery, and on the varicoloured birds in their invisible cage of curtain-jets of air. Across the park there tumbled a narrow stream of free fresh water; today its level had fallen so that the concrete sides of its bed were revealed halfway down

A year ago—a lifetime ago—when the real world had been still alive, Derron Odegard had not been one to spend much time in the appreciation of nature. Oh, a hike now and then in the fresh air. But he had been concentrating on finishing his schooling and getting settled down to the labours of the professional historian. He had centred his life in texts and films and tapes, and the usual academic schemes for academic advancement. Even his hikes and holidays had taken him to places of historic significance...with an effort that had become reflex, he forced the image of the girl he had loved once more from his thoughts.

A year ago, a historian's career had been a prospect filled with excitement, made electric by the first hints from the physicists that the quirks of Sirgol's unique spacetime might prove susceptive to manipulation, that humanity on Sirgol might be granted a first-hand look at much of its own past. Only a year ago, the berserker-war had seemed remote; a terrible thing of course, but afflicting only other worlds, light-years away. Decades had passed since the Earthmen had brought warning, and Sirgol's planetary defences had been decades in the building, a routine part of life's background for a young man finishing his schooling.

It occurred to Derron now, as a trivial truism, that in the past year he had learned more about history than he had in all the years of study that had gone before. Not that it was doing him any good. He thought now that when the last moment of history came on Sirgol, if he could know it was the last, he would get away if he could to one of these little parks with a small bottle of wine he had been saving. He would finish history by drinking whatever number of toasts history allowed, to whatever dead and dying things seemed to him most worthy of mourning.

The tension of the day's watch was just beginning to drain from his fingers into the handworn bark of the railing, and he had actually forgotten the recent explosion, when the first of the wounded came stumbling into the park below.

The first came out of a narrow grass-level entrance, a man with his uniform jacket gone and the rest of his clothing torn and blackened. One of his bared arms was burnt and raw and swollen. He walked quickly, half-blindly, among the trees, and then like an actor in some wilderness drama fell full length at the edge of the artificial brook and drank from it ravenously.

Next from the same entrance came another man, older, more sedentary-looking. Probably some kind of clerk or administrator, though at the distance Derron could not make out his insignia. This man was not visibly wounded, but he moved into the park as if he was lost. Now and then he raised his hands to his ears; he might be deaf, or just wondering if his head was still on.

A pudgy woman entered, moaning in bewilderment, using first one hand and then the other to hold the flap of her torn scalp in place. After her another woman. A steady trickle of the suffering and maimed was flowing from the little entrance at grass level, spilling into the false peace of the park and defiling it with the swelling chorus of their querulous voices.

From somewhere down the passages came authoritarian yells, and then the whine and rumble of heavy machinery. Damage Control was on the job promptly, for rescue and emergency repair. The walking wounded were obviously being sent to the park to get them out from under foot while more urgent matters were handled. By now there were a couple of dozen sufferers wandering over the grass or lying on it, their groans demanding of the trees why the missile had had to get through today, why it had had to come to them.

Among the wounded there walked a slender girl of eighteen or twenty, clad in the remnants of a simple paper uniform dress. She stopped, leaning against a tree as if she could walk no further. The way her dress was torn. . . .

Derron turned away from the railing, squeezing his eyes shut in a spasm of self-disgust. He had suddenly seen himself, standing here like some ancient tyrant remotely entertained by others' pain, condescending to lust with a critical eye. One of these days, and soon, he would have to decide whether he was really still on the side of the human race or not.

There was a stairway handy, and he skipped down it to the ground level of the park. The badly burned man was bathing his raw arm in the cool running water, and others were drinking. No one seemed to have stopped breathing, or to be bleeding to death. The girl looked as if she might fall away from her supporting tree at any moment.

Pulling off his jacket as he went to her, Derron wrapped her in the garment and eased her away from the tree. "Where are you hurt?"

She shook her head and said something incoherent. Her face was pale enough for her to be in shock, so he tried to get her to sit down. She wouldn't, and so the two of them did a little off-balance dance while he held her up. She was a tall, slim girl, and under ordinary conditions she would be lovely...no, not lovely, or anyway not standard-pretty. But good to look at certainly. Her hair, like most women's these days, was cut in the short simple style promoted by the government. She was wearing no jewellery or make-up at all, which was a bit unusual.

She soon came out of her daze enough to look with bewilderment at the jacket which had been wrapped around her. "You're an officer," she said in a low blurry voice, her eyes focusing on the collar insignia.

"In a very small way. Now hadn't you better lie down somewhere?"

"No...I've been trying to get home...or somewhere. Can't you tell me where I am? What's going on?" Her voice was rising.

"I believe there was a missile strike. Here now, this insignia of mine is supposed to be a help with the girls, so sit down at least, won't you?"

She wouldn't, and they danced a few more steps. "No. First I have to find out...I don't know who I am, or where, or why!"

"I don't know those things about myself." That was the most honest communication he had spoken to anyone in a considerable time. More people, passers-by and medics, were running into the park now, adding to the general confusion as they tried to help the wounded. Becoming gradually more aware of her surroundings, the girl looked wildly around at all this activity, and clung to Derron's arm.

"All right, young lady, since you seem determined to walk I'm going to take you to the hospital. There's one not far from here, just down the elevator. Come along."

The girl was willing enough to walk beside him, holding his arm. "What's your name?" he asked her as they boarded the elevator. The other people aboard stared at the dazed girl wearing his jacket.

"I...don't know!" Finding her name gone, she became really frightened. Her hand went to her throat, but no dog-tag depended there. Many people didn't like to wear them, and disregarded the regulation requiring it. "Where are you taking me?"

"I told you, to a hospital. You need some looking after." He

18

would have liked to give a wilder answer, for their staring fellow-passengers' benefit.

Down at Operations level he led the girl off the elevator. A few more steps brought them to an emergency entrance to the hospital complex. Other casualties from the explosion, stretcher cases, were arriving now and the emergency room was crowded. An elderly nurse started to take Derron's jacket off the girl, and what was left of her own clothing peeled away with it. The girl squealed faintly and the nurse re-wrapped with a brisk motion. "You just come back for this jacket tomorrow, young man."

"Gladly." And then the pressure of stretcher-bearers and other busy people was such that he could do no more than wave goodbye to the girl as he was forced slowly out into the corridor. He disentangled himself from the crowd and walked away smiling, almost laughing to himself over the nurse and the jacket, as if it had been a great joke. It was a while since he had had a thought that seemed worth smiling at.

He was still smiling faintly as he ducked into the Time Operations complex, to pick up the spare jacket he kept in his locker in the sentries' ready room. There was nothing new on the bulletin board. He thought, not for the first time, of applying for a transfer, to some job that didn't require sitting still for six hours of deadly strain a day. But it seemed that those who didn't apply were just about as likely to be transferred as those who did.

Naturally the girl's husband or lover would probably show up before tomorrow to claim her. Of course—a girl like that. Well, he would hope someone showed up for her—a sister or a brother, perhaps.

He went into the nearby officers' gym and got into a handball game with his old classmate Chan Amling, who was now a captain in Historical Research Section; Amling was not one to play without betting, and Derron won an ersatz soft drink which he preferred not to collect. The talk in the gym was mostly about Time Operations' first victory; when someone brought up the subject of the missile strike, Derron said no more than that he had seen some of the wounded.

After showering, Derron and Amling and a couple of others went to a bar on Housing Level that Amling favoured. Major Lukas, the chief historical psychologist in Time Operations, was established there in a booth, holding forth on the psychic and other attributes of some new girls at a local uplevel dive called the Red Garter. There were some areas in which private enterprise still flourished with a minimum of governmental interference.

Amling bet with the others on darts, on dice, and on something having to do with the Red Garter girls. Derron wasn't listening too closely, though for a change he was smiling and joking a little. He had one drink, his usual maximum, and relaxed for a while amid the social noise.

In the local officers' mess he ate his dinner with a better appetite than usual. When at last he reached his cubicle, he kicked off his shoes and stretched out on his cot, and for once was sound asleep before he could even consider taking a pill.

After coming stiffly awake in the middle of the night, then getting undressed and going properly to bed, he still awoke somewhat ahead of schedule and feeling well rested. The little clock on his cubicle wall read o-six-thirty hours, Planet-wide Emergency Time. This morning none of Time's aspects weighed on him very heavily. Certainly he had enough of the mysterious dimension at his disposal to let him stop at the hospital for a while before going on duty.

Carrying yesterday's jacket over his arm, he followed a nurse's directions and found the girl seated in a patients' lounge, which at this time of the morning she had pretty much to herself. She was planted directly in front of the television, frowning with naive-looking concentration at Channel Gung-Ho, as the government's exhortation channel was popularly known. Today the girl was wearing a plain new paper dress, and hospital slippers.

At the sound of Derron's step she turned her head quickly, then smiled and got to her feet. "Oh, it's you! It's a good feeling to recognize someone."

Derron took the hand she was holding out. "It's a good feeling to be recognized. You're looking much better."

She thanked Derron for his help and he protested that it had been nothing. She turned off the television sound and they sat down to talk. He introduced himself.

Her smile vanished. "I wish I could tell you my name."

"I know, I talked with the nurse . . . they say your amnesia is persisting, but outside of that you're doing fine."

"Yes, I feel fine outside of that one little detail. I guess I wasn't physically hurt at all. And I have a new name, of sorts. Lisa Gray. For the sake of their hospital records they had to tag me with something, next off some list they keep handy. Evidently a fair number of people go blank in the upper story these days and have to be re-named. And they say so many records, fingerprints and things, were lost when the surface was evacuated."

"Lisa's a nice name. I think it suits you."

"Thank you, sir." She managed to sound almost carefree for a moment.

Derron considered. "You know I've heard that being in the path of a missile, being run over by the probability-wave before it materializes, can cause amnesia. It's a little like being dropped into the deep past, sort of wipes the slate clean."

The girl nodded. "Yes, the doctors think that's what happened to me yesterday. They tell me that when the missile hit I was with a group of people being brought down from an upper level that's being evacuated. I suppose if I had any next of kin with me, they were blown to pieces along with our records. Nobody's come looking for me."

It was a story common enough on Sirgol to be boring, but this time Derron could feel the pain in it. In sympathy he changed the subject. "Have you had your breakfast yet?"

"Yes. There's a little automat right here if you want something. Maybe I could use some more fruit juice."

In a minute Derron was back, carrying one paper cup of the orange-coloured liquid called fruit juice, one cup of tea, and a couple of the standard sweet-rolls. Lisa was again studying the television version of the war; the commentator's stentorian voice was still turned mercifully low.

Derron laid out his cargo on a low table and pulled his own chair closer. Glancing at Lisa's puzzled expression, he asked: "Do you remember much about the war?"

"Amost nothing . . . I guess that part of my memory really was wiped clean. What are these berserkers? I know they're something terrible, but . . ."

"Well, they're machines." Derron sipped his tea. "Some of them are bigger than any spaceships that we or any other

Earth-descended men have ever built. Others come in different shapes and sizes, but all of them are deadly. The first of them were constructed ages ago, by some race we've never met, to fight in some war we've never heard of.

"They were programmed to destroy life anywhere they could find it, and they've come only the Holy One knows how far, doing just that." Derron had begun in a conversational tone, and his voice was still quiet, but now the words seemed welling up from an inexhaustible spring of bitterness. "Sometimes men have beaten them in battle, but some of them have always survived. The survivors hide out on some unexplored rocks, around some dark star, and they build more of their kind, with improvements. And then they come back. They just go on and on, like death itself . . ."

"No," said Lisa, unwilling to have it so.

"I'm sorry, I didn't mean to start raving. Not so early in the morning, anyway." He smiled faintly. He supposed he had no reasonable excuse for unloading his weighted soul onto this girl. But once things started pouring out . . . "We on Sirgol were alive, and so the berserkers had to kill us. But since they're only machines, why it's all only an accident, sort of a cosmic joke. An act of the Holy One, as people used to put it. We have no one to take revenge on." His voice choked in his tight throat; he gulped at his tea and pushed the cup away.

Lisa asked: "Won't men come from other planets to help us?"

He sighed. His voice became slower. "Some of them are fighting berserkers near their own systems. A really big relief fleet would have to be put together to do us any good, while of course politics must still be played among the stars as usual. Oh, I suppose help will be sent eventually."

The television commentator was droning on aggressively about men's brilliant defensive victories on the moon, while an appropriate videotape was being shown. The chief satellite of Sirgol was said to much resemble the moon of Earth; long before either men or berserkers had existed, its round face had been pocked by impact craters into an awed expression. But during the last year the face of Sirgol's moon had vanished under a rash of new impacts, along with practically all of the human defenders there.

"I think help will come to us in time," said Lisa.

22

In time for what? Derron wondered. "I suppose so," he said, and felt that he was lying.

Now the television was presenting a scene on Sirgol's dayside. Under a sky of savage blue—a little atmosphere was left—cracked mudflats stretched away to a levelled horizon. Nothing lived. Nothing moved but a few thin whirlwinds of yellow-grey dust. Rising gleaming from the dried mud in the middle distance were the bright steel bones of some invading berserker device, smashed and twisted last tenday or last month by some awesome energy of defence. Another victory for the droning voice to try to magnify.

Lisa turned away from the desolate display. "I have a few memories left, of beautiful things on the surface. Not like that."

"Yes. There were some beautiful things."

"Tell me."

"Well." He smiled faintly. "Do you prefer to hear about man's marvellous creations, or the wonders of nature?"

"Things men made, I suppose . . . oh, I don't know. Man is a part of nature, isn't he? And so the things he makes are, too, in a way."

There rose before his mind's eye the image of a cathedral-temple towering on a hill, and a sunburst of stained glass . . . but that would not bear remembering. He said: "I don't know if we can be considered a part of nature on this planet or not. You remember how peculiar the spacetime around Sirgol is?"

"You mean about the First Men coming here—but I don't think I ever really understood the scientific explanation. Tell me."

"Well." Derron put on something of the professional historian's manner that he had never had much chance to use. "Our sun looks much like any other G-type star that has an Earth-type planet. But in our case appearances are deceiving. Oh, in ordinary human life, time is the same as elsewhere. And interstellar ships that travel faster than light can enter and leave our system—if they take precautions.

"The first starship to arrive here was an explorer from Earth. Her crew of course had no way of knowing about our tricky spacetime. While approaching an uninhabited Sirgol, their ship accidentally dropped back through about twenty thousand years—an accident that could have happened no-where else in the known universe.

"Only on Sirgol is time travel possible, and then only under certain conditions. One of these conditions seems to be that anyone who goes back more than about five hundred years undergoes enough mental devolution to wipe his memory out. Of course that happened to the Earthmen on the explorer. Her crew became the First Men—and the First Women, too, of course—of our mythology. After dropping twenty thousand years they must have had no memories left at all. They must have crawled around like babies after their ship landed itself."

"How could they ever have survived?"

"We don't really know. Instinct, and luck. The grace of God, religious people say. We can't get a look at the First Men, even with spy devices, and fortunately the berserkers can't reach them either. The first humans on the planet of course form an evolutionary peduncle, a true new beginning. And as such they tend to be invisible, unfindable from the future, no matter what techniques are employed."

"I thought evolution was just a matter of random mutations, some of which work out and some don't." Lisa nibbled at a sweetroll, listening carefully.

"There's a good deal more than that involved. You see, matter has organisational energies, as well as the more obvious kinds. The movement of all matter through time is towards greater complexity, raising level after level of organisation higher and higher above chaos—the human brain supposedly represents one of the peaks, to date, of this process. Or this is the optimistic view most scientists say they hold...it doesn't seem to include the berserkers. Anyway, where was I?"

"The First People had landed."

"Oh yes. Well, they kept on surviving somehow, and multi-plying. Over thousands of years they built up civilizations from scratch. When the second exploring ship from Earth arrived here, about ten years Earth-time after the first, we had achieved a planet-wide government and were just getting started on space travel ourselves. In fact the second Earth ship was attracted by signals from some of our early interplanetary probes. The crew of the second ship approached more cautiously than the first ship had, realized they were facing a tricky patch of spacetime, and landed successfully.

"Pretty soon the men from Earth had figured out what had happened to the crew of the first ship, and were saluting us as their descendants. They also brought us warning of the berserkers. Took some of our people to other systems and gave them a glimpse of what the war against the machines was like. Of course the people of Earth and other worlds were pleased to have four hundred million new allies, and they deluged us with advice on planet-weapons and fortifications, and we spent the next eighty years getting ready to defend ourselves. And then about a year ago the berserker fleet came. End of lesson, end of history."

Lisa did not seem dismayed by the end of history. She drank some of the so-called juice as if she liked it, and prompted: "What do you do now, Derron?"

"Oh, various odd jobs in Time Operations. You see, the berserker offensive in present-time is stalled. They can't pry us out of these deep caves, and they can't build themselves a base on the planet, or even hold a beachhead on the surface, while we're here. They've discovered the time travel bit, so of course now they're using it to try to get at us through our past. In their first attack along that line they tried to slaughter everything alive, in true berserker style, but we stopped that rather easily. So their next attempt will probably be more subtle. They'll kill some important individual, or do something else to delay some vital step in our history. Perhaps the invention of the wheel or something like that. Then succeeding steps in our development will automatically be delayed. We'd be in the Middle Ages, perhaps, when the second explorer from Earth arrived. No radio signals to guide the Earthmen to us. Or if they found us anyway, we'd have no technological base and no modern industry to build ourselves defences. Earth and other planets have enough trouble defending themselves. Therefore we'd be unprotected when the berserkers came. Therefore today no stubborn resistance from the caves—we'd all be either dead or non-existent, it's a nice philosophical problem which."

"Oh! But you'll be able to stop their time-attacks. I'm sure you will!"

Pour out what bitter hopelessness you might, there was nothing left at last to do with this girl but smile at her and wish her well, and Derron found himself smiling, after two or three false starts. Then he glanced at the version of Time he wore on his wrist. "If it all depends on me, I guess I'd better go and start my day's heroic fighting."

Today the briefing officer for Derron's sentry-shift was Colonel Borss, who as usual handled the job with the sombre expectancy of a Scriptural prophet.

"As we all know, yesterday's defensive action was a tactical success," the colonel admitted to begin with. In the semi-darkness of the briefing room his pointer skipped across the glowing symbols on the huge display he had prepared. Then Derron, seated near the front, could see the colonel smile as he continued: "But, strategically speaking, we must admit that the situation has somewhat deteriorated."

It soon became evident that the cause of the colonel's gloomy smile was the existence of the enemy staging area, still not accurately located but known to be somewhere more than twenty-one thousand years down. "After the enemy has made three more sorties up from there, three more breakthroughs into real-time, we'll have three vectors to trace back, enough to give us a positive fix on his staging area. We'll smash it with a few missiles, and that will kill his entire Time Operations programme."

The colonel paused before delivering his punch line. "Of course, we have first to deal with the little problem of repelling three more attacks."

The audience of junior officers dutifully made faint laughing sounds. Colonel Borss switched his display screen to show a glowing, tree-like shape, which the labels showed to be a type of graph of human history on Sirgol.

He tapped with his pointer far down on the tree's trunk, where it was still a slender shoot growing up out of question marks. "We rather expect that the first of the three attacks will fall here. Somewhere near the First Men."

Matt, sometimes also named Lion-Hunter, felt the afternoon sun warm on his bare shoulders as he turned away from the last familiar landmarks, putting behind him the territory in which he had lived all his twenty-five years.

To get a better view of the land ahead, into which he and the rest of The People were fleeing, he climbed up now onto a shoulder-high rock that stood beside the faint game trail they were following. The little band of The People, now no more in number than a man's fingers and toes, went shuffling past Matt at a steady pace, walking in a thin and wide-spaced file. They were of all ages. Such garments as they wore were bark or leather, and besides their scanty clothing they had little enough to burden them. On this journey no one was hanging back, no one trying to argue the others into stopping or turning around.

The land ahead wavered with the spirits of heat. From atop the rock Matt could see swamps in that direction, and barren hills. Nothing very inviting. There might be strange dangers as well as familiar ones in the unfamiliar land ahead, but everyone had agreed in council that nothing there was likely to be as terrible as that from which they fled—the new beasts, lions with flesh of shiny stone, lions who could not be hurt by the stones or arrows of men, who came killing by day and night, who could kill with only a glance of their fiery eyes.

In the past two days, ten of The People had been slain by the stone-lions. And the survivors had been able to do nothing but hide, hardly daring even to look for a puddle from which to drink, or to pull up a root to eat.

Slung over Matt's shoulder was the only bow now left to the survivors of The People. The other bows had been burnt or broken along with the men who had tried to use them in defence against a stone-lion. Tomorrow, Matt thought, he would try hunting meat in the new country. No one was carrying any food now. Some of the young ones wailed now and then with hunger, until the women pinched their noses and mouths to keep them quiet.

The file of The People had passed Matt now. He ran his eye along the line of familiar backs, found their number one short, and was frowning as he hopped down from his rock.

A few strides brought him up to those in the rear of the march. "Where is Dart?" he asked. It was not that Matt had any idea of controlling the comings and goings of the members of the band, though he more than anyone else was their leader. It was just that he wanted to know everything that was going on, with the stone-lions behind them and an unknown land ahead.

Dart was an orphan, but now too big to be any longer

considered a child, and so none of the other adults were especially concerned.

"He kept saying how hungry he was," a woman said. "And then a little while ago when you were in the rear he ran on toward those swampy woods ahead. I suppose looking for food."

Derron was just buying Lisa some lunch—from the automat in the patients' lounge, since she was still hospitalized for observation—when the public address speakers began to broadcast a list of Time Operations men who were to report for duty at once. He heard his name included.

He scooped up a sandwich to eat as he ran, and bade Lisa a hasty goodbye. Quick as he was, most of the group of twenty-four men were already assembled when he reached the room to which they had been summoned. Colonel Borss was pacing back and forth impatiently, discouraging questions.

Soon after Derron's arrival, the last man on the list came in, and the colonel could begin.

"Gentlemen, the first assault has come just about as predicted. The keyhole has not yet been pinpointed, but it's approximately three hundred years after the most probable time of the First Men.

"As in the previous attack, we are faced with six enemy machines breaking into real-time. But in this case the machines are not flyers, or at least they seem not to be operating in an airborne mode. Probably they are anti-personnel devices that move on legs or rollers; certainly they will be invulnerable to any means of self-defence possessed by the Neolithic population.

"We anticipate great difficulty in finding the keyhole, because the destructive changes caused directly by this attack are quantitatively much less than those we saw last time. This time the berserkers are evidently concentrating on some historically important small group or individual. Just who in the invaded area is so important we don't know yet, but we will. Any questions on what I've said so far? Then here's Colonel Nilos, to brief you on your part in our planned counter-measures."

Nilos, an earnest young man with a rasping voice, came straight to the point. "You twenty-four men all have high scores in training on the master-slave androids. No one has any

28

real combat experience with them yet, but you soon will. I'm authorized to tell you that you're all relieved of all other duties as of now."

Well, I wanted a transfer, thought Derron, leaning back in his chair with a mental shrug. Around him the reactions ranged from joy to dismay, in muted exclamations. The other men were all noncoms or junior officers like himself, drawn from various sections in Operations. He knew a few of them, but only slightly.

The various reactions of pleasure or distress at the change of duty and the imminence of combat continued as the two dozen men were conducted to a nearby ready room where they were left to wait idly for some minutes; and as they were taken by elevator down to Operations Stage Three, on the lowest and most heavily defended level yet excavated.

Stage Three, a great echoing cave the size of a large aircraft hangar, was spanned by a catwalk at a good distance above the floor. From this catwalk, looking like space-suits on puppet-strings, were suspended the two dozen master-units that Derron and the other operators were to wear. In a neat corresponding rank on the floor below the masters stood their slaves, their metal bodies taller and broader than those of the men, so that they dwarfed the technicians who now laboured at giving them the final touches of combat-readiness.

In small rooms at the side of Stage Three, the operators were given individual briefings, shown maps of the terrain where they were to be dropped, and provided with an outline of the scanty information available on the Neolithic semi-nomads they were to protect. Then after a last brief medical check, the operators were dressed in leotards and marched up onto the catwalk.

At this point the word was passed down from high authority to hold things up. For a few moments no one seemed to know the cause of the delay; then a huge screen at one side of the Stage lit up, filled with an image of the bald massive head of the Planetary Commander himself.

"Men . . ." boomed the familiar amplified voice. Then the image paused, frowning off-camera. "What's that?" it shouted after a moment. "Operations has them *waiting* for me? Tell him to get on with the job! I can give pep-talks any time! What does he think——?"

The Planetary Commander's voice was still rising when it was cut off with his picture; Derron was left with the impression that Number One still had a lot to say, and indifferent as Derron was to the progress of his own military career, he was glad it was not being said to him.

Things in Stage Three promptly got moving again. A pair of technicians came to help Derron into his assigned master-unit, a process like climbing down into a heavy diving-suit suspended on cables. The master was an enormously awkward thing to wear, until the servo-power was turned on. Then the thick body and heavy limbs at once became delicately responsive to their wearer's least movement.

"Slave power coming on," said a voice in Derron's helmet. And a moment later it seemed to all his senses that he had been transported from the master down into the body of the slave-unit standing below it on the floor. As the control of its movements passed over to him, the slave started gradually to lean to one side, and he moved its foot as naturally as his own to maintain balance. Tilting back his head, he could look up through the slave's eyes to see the master-unit, himself inside, maintaining the same attitude on its complex suspension.

"Form a file for launching," was the next command in his helmet. The slaves' metal feet echoed on the hard floor of the cavernous chamber as the squad of them faced left into line. Human technicians who seemed to have suddenly shrunk scurried to get out of the way. At the head of the line of metalmen the floor of the Stage blossomed out suddenly into a bright mercurial disk.

"...four, three, two, one, launch!"

With immense and easy power the line of tall bodies ran toward the circle on the dark floor, disappearing in turn as they reached it. The figure ahead of Derron jumped, and vanished. Then he himself, in proxy, leaped out over the silvery spot.

His metal feet came down on grass, and he staggered briefly on uneven ground. He was standing in shadowy daylight in the midst of a leafy forest.

He checked a compass set in the slave's wrist, and then moved at once to a place from which he could get a good look at the sun. It was low in the western sky, which indicated that he had missed his planned moment of arrival by some hours—if not by days or months or years. He reported the apparent error at once, subvocalizing to keep the slave's speaker silent.

"Start coursing then, Odegard," said one of the controllers. "We'll try to get a fix on you."

"Understand."

Derron began to walk a spiral path through the woods. Of course while doing this he kept alert for any sign of the enemy, or of the people he had been sent to protect. But the main purpose of this coursing manoeuvre was to splash up a few waves—to create disturbances in the historical course of the plant and animal lifelines about him, disturbances which a skilled sentry some twenty thousand years in the future would hopefully be able to see and pinpoint.

After Derron had walked a gradually enlarging spiral for some ten minutes, alarming perhaps a hundred small animals, crushing perhaps a thousand unseen insects underfoot, and bruising uncountable leaves of grass and tree, the impersonal controller's voice spoke again.

"All right, Odegard, we've got you spotted. You're slightly off spatially but in the right direction to let you catch up with your people. You'll need to do some catching up because you're between four and five hours late. The sun's going down, right?"

"It is."

"All right, then, bear about two hundred degrees from magnetic north. If you walk that course for a quarter of an hour you should be very near your people."

"Understand." Instead of having a chance to scout the area before his people walked through it, he would just be hurrying to catch them before something else caught them. Derron started off at a brisk pace, checking his compass regularly to keep the slave going in a straight line. Ahead of him, the wooded land sloped gradually downward into a swampy area. Beyond the further edge of swamp, several hundred metres from his present position, there rose low rocky hills.

"Odegard, we're getting indications of another disturbing factor, right there on top of you. Sorry we can't give you a good bearing on it. It's almost certainly one of the berserkers."

"Understand." This kind of work was more to Derron's taste than being immobilized in a sentry's chair; but still the weight of forty million lives was back on his neck again, as deadly as ever.

Some minutes passed. Derron's progress had slowed, for he was having to keep a lookout in all directions while planning a good path for the heavy slave-unit to take through the marshy ground. And then all at once he heard trouble, plain and unmistakable—it sounded like a child screaming in terror.

"Operations, I'm onto something."

The scream came again and again. The slave-unit's ears were keen, and directionally accurate. Derron changed course slightly and began to run, leaping the unit over the softest-looking spots of ground, striving for both speed and silence.

After he had run for half a minute he slid as silently as possible to a halt. A stone's throw ahead, a boy of about twelve was up in a treetop, clinging tightly to the thin upper trunk with both arms and legs but still in danger of being shaken down. Every time his yelling ceased for a moment, another sharp tremor would run up the trunk and set him off again. The tree's lower trunk was thick, but still it was being shaken like a sapling by something concealed in the bush around its base. There was no animal in this forest with strength like that; it would be the berserker machine in the bush, using the boy as bait, hoping that his cries would bring the adults of his group.

Derron stepped slowly forward. But before he could tell on which side of the tree the berserker was, and take aim, it spotted the slave-outfit. Out of the bush a pinkish laser beam came stabbing, to gouge a fireworks display from the armour covering the slave's mid-section. Levelling the laser beam before it like a lance, heaving bushes and saplings out of its way, the berserker charged. Derron caught a glimpse of something metallic and low, four-legged, wide and fast-moving as a groundcar. He snapped open his jaw, pressing down inside his helmet on the trigger of his own laser weapon. From the centre of the slave's forehead a pale thin shaft of light crackled out, aimed automatically at the spot where Derron's eyes were focused.

The slave-unit's beam smote the charging machine amid the knobs of metal that made it seem to have a face, and glanced off to explode a small tree into a cloud of flame and steam.

The shot might have done damage, for the enemy broke off its rush in midstride and dove for cover behind a hillock, a grass-tufted hump of ground less than five feet high.

Two officers in Operations, who were evidently both monitoring the video signal from the slave, began simultaneously to give Derron orders and advice. Even if they had gone about it sensibly, he had no time now to do anything but go his own way. Somewhat surprised at his own aggressiveness, he found himself running the slave-unit in a crouch around the tiny hill.

He wanted the fight to be over quickly, one way or the other. He charged at top speed, yelling wordlessly inside his helmet as he fired his laser. The berserker burst into his view, crouched like a metal lion, squat and immensely powerful. If there had been a spare moment in which to hesitate, Derron might have flinched away, for in spite of all his training the illusion was very strong that he was actually about to hurl his own tender flesh upon the waiting monster.

As it was, he had no time to flinch. With all the inertia of its metal mass the slave ran at full speed into the crouching berserker. The trees in the swamp quivered.

A few seconds' experience were enough to convince Derron that the decision to use anthropomorphic fighting machines in this operation had been a great blunder. Wrestling was a tactic not likely to succeed against a machine of equal or superior power, and one not limited in the speed of its reactions by the slowness of protoplasmic nerves. For all the slave-unit's fusion-powered strength, which Operations had envisioned as rending the enemy limb from limb, Derron could do no more than hang on desperately, gripping the berserker in a kind of half-nelson while it bucked and twisted like a wild loadbeast to throw him off.

Once the fight started it seemed to Derron that every authority in Operations was looking over his shoulder, and that most of them had something to say about it. Voices in Derron's ears shouted orders and abuse at him and one another. Some of them were probably trying to get others off his back, but he had no time to hear them anyway. The green forest was spinning round him faster than his eyes and brain could sort it out. In a dizzily detached fraction of a second he could notice how his feet flew uselessly on the ends of his metal legs, breaking down small trees as the monster whirled him. He tried to turn his head to bring the cyclops' eye of his laser to bear, but now one of the berserker's forelimbs was gripping the slave's neck, holding the slave's head immobile. He kept trying desperately to get a more solid grip for his own steel arms round the berserker's thick neck, but then his grip was broken and he flew.

Before the slave could even bounce, the berserker was on top of it, far faster and more violent than any maddened bull. Derron fired his laser wildly. The dizziness of the spinning, and now the panicky sensation of being painlessly trampled and battered, raised in him a giddy urge to laughter. In a moment more the fight would be lost and he would be able to give up.

The berserker tossed him once again. And then it was running away, fleeing from Derron's wildly slashing sword of light. As lightly as a deer the squat machine leaped away among the trees and vanished from Derron's sight.

Dizzily he tried to sit up, on the peculiar sandy slope where he had been flung. In doing so he at once discovered why the berserker had chosen to retreat; some important part had been broken in the slave, so that its legs now trailed as limp and useless as those of a man with a broken spine. But as the slave's laser still worked, and its powerful arms could still do damage, the berserker's computer-brain had decided to break off the fight. The berserker saw no reason to trade zaps with a crippled but still dangerous antagonist, not when it could be busy at its basic programme of killing people.

The Operations voices had their final say.

"Odegard, why in the——?"

"In the Holy One's name, Odegard, what do you think——?"

"Odegard, why didn't you——? Oh, do what you can!"

With a click they were all gone from his helmet, leaving their disgust behind. He had the dazed impression that they were all hurrying away in a jealous group, to descend like a cloud of scavenger-birds upon some other victim. If his experience since taking the field was anywhere near typical, the foul-up of the whole operation must be approaching the monumental stage, that stage where avoidance of blame would begin to take precedence in a good many minds.

Anyway, he was still in the field, now with half a unit to work with. His disgust was mainly with himself. Gone now was the wish to get things settled quickly, one way or the other. Even his dread of responsibility was gone, at least for the moment. Right now all he wanted was another chance at the enemy.

Holding the slave propped with its arms into a sitting position, he looked about him. He was halfway down the conical side of a soggy sandpit which at the top was ten or fifteen metres across. Nothing grew inside the pit; outside, the nearby trees were nearly all in bad shape, those that had escaped being broken in the wrestling match were blackened and smoking from his wildly-aimed laser.

What had happened to the boy?

Working his arms like a swimmer, Derron churned his way uphill through the sand to a spot from which he could see over the rim of the pit. He could recognize, a short distance away, the tall tree in which the youngster had been clinging for his life; but he was not in sight now, living or dead.

In a sudden little sand-slide the crippled slave slid once more down the tricky slope toward the watery mess that filled the bottom of the funnel.

Funnel?

Derron at last recognized the place where the slave-unit had been thrown. It was the trap of a poison-digger, a species of large carnivore exterminated on Sirgol in early historical times. Looking down now at the bottom of the pit, Derron met the gaze of two greyish eyes, set in a large lump of head that floated just half above the surface of the water.

Matt was standing just behind the boy Dart, while both of them peered very cautiously through the bushes toward the poison-digger's trap. The rest of The People were a few hundred yards away, resting in the concealment of some undergrowth while they scratched up a few roots and grubs to eat.

Matt could just catch glimpses, above the rim of the funnel, of what seemed to be a head. It was certainly not the poison-digger's head, but a shape as bald and smoothly curved as a drop of water.

"I think it is a stone-lion," Matt whispered very softly.

"Ah no," whispered Dart. "This is the big man I told you about, the stone-man. Ah, what a fight he and the stone-lion had! But I didn't wait to see the end of it, I jumped from the tree and ran while I could."

Matt hesitated, and then decided to risk a closer look. Motioning with his head for Dart to follow, he bent down and crept forward. From behind another bush they could see down into the pit, and Matt was just in time to observe something that made him gasp silently in amazement. Poison-Digger, who could master any creature once it had fallen into his pit, reared up from his slime and struck. And the stone-man simply slapped Digger's nose with casual force, like someone swatting a child. And with a howl like the cry of a punished child, the Bad One splashed down under his water again!

The man of shiny stone muttered to himself. His words were filled with power and feeling, but in a tongue unknown to Matt. He slapped at his legs, which lay twisted as if they were dead, and then with his big arms he started trying to dig his way up out of the pit. Stone-man made the sand fly, and Matt thought he might eventually get himself out, but it looked like a very hard struggle.

"Now do you believe me?" Dart was whispering fiercely. "He did fight the stone-lion, I saw him!"

"Yes, yes, I can believe it." Still crouching and keeping out of sight of the pit, Matt led the young one away, back toward the others of the band. He supposed that a fight between two such beings might have accounted for all the burnt and broken trees that had puzzled him earlier, and for all the noise that The People had heard. Now, while leading Dart away from the pit, Matt looked hopefully among the bushes for a huge shiny corpse. A dead stone-lion was one sight Matt wanted very much to see—it might help blot out another picture that would not leave his mind, the picture of what a stone-lion had done to his two young wives.

Huddling under bushes with the rest of the band, Matt talked things over with the more intelligent adults. "I want to approach this stone-man," he said, "and try to help him."

"Why?"

Finding the words to explain why was not easy. For one thing Matt was eager to join forces, if he could, with any power that was able to fight against a stone-lion. But there was more to it than that, for this particular stone-man did not look capable of much more fighting.

The others listened to Matt, but kept muttering doubtfully. Finally the oldest woman of The People took from her lizard-skin pouch (in which she also carried the seed of fire) the finger bones of her predecessor in office. Three times she shook the bones, and threw them on the muddy ground, and studied the pattern in which they fell. But she could not see the stone-man in the bones, and she could offer no advice.

The more he thought about it, the more determined Matt became. "I'm going to try to help the stone-man. If he does turn out to be hostile, he can't chase us on his dead legs."

The slave-unit's ears picked up the approach of the whole band of The People, though they were being very quiet.

"I'm getting some company," Derron subvocalized. He got no immediate reply from any of the too-many chiefs who had been overseeing him before; which suited him just as well for the moment.

The People drew near, and the bolder among them peered cautiously from behind bush and tree trunk at the slave-unit. When they saw its head was raised, looking at them, they stepped one at a time out of concealment, showing weaponless hands. Derron imitated the gesture as well as he could; he needed one hand to support the slave in a sitting position.

The People seemed to slowly gain confidence from the slave's peaceful gestures, its quiescence, and probably most of all from its obviously crippled condition. Soon the whole band had come out into the open, and stood whispering among themselves as they peered curiously down into the pit.

"Anybody listening?" Derron subvocalized. "I've got a crowd of people here. Get me a linguist?"

Since the start of Time Operations a desperate effort had been made to learn as many as possible of the languages and dialects of Sirgol's past. Disguised microphones and video pick-ups had been carried on spy-devices to many places and times in the past where there were people to be studied. The pro-gramme of study had been pushed as hard as possible, but the magnitude of the job was overwhelming. In the Modern world there were just two people who had managed to learn something of the speech of these Neolithic semi-nomads, and those two were very busy people today.

"Odegard!" When response did come, it took the form of a blast in his helmet that made Derron wince. The voice did not identify itself, but sounded like that of Colonel Borss. "Don't let those people get away from you! Even if your unit's crippled, it can offer them some protection."

"Understand." Derron sighed, sub-subvocally. "How about getting me a linguist?"

"We're trying to get you one. You're in a vital area there... stand guard over those people until we can get another unit to the spot!"

"Understood." Things were tough in the berserker-ridden Neolithic today. But he might after all be better off sealed up in his master-unit than out in the foul-up and confusion that must be engulfing the Section.

"Anyone that size is bound to eat a lot of food," one of the older men was complaining to Matt.

"With his dead legs," Matt answered, "I don't suppose he'll live long enough to eat very much." Matt was trying to talk some of the braver men into giving him a hand in pulling the stone-man up out of the trap. Stone-man seemed to be waiting with some confidence of getting help.

The man debating against Matt cheerfully switched arguments. "If he's not going to live long, there's no use trying to help him. Anyway he's not one of The People."

"No, he's not. But still..." Matt continued to search for new words, new ways of thought. He would help the stone-man alone if he had to. In arguing he was trying to make his feelings clear to himself as well as to the others. He saw this strange being who had tried to help Dart as a part of some larger order, to which The People also belonged; as if there could be a band, a tribe-of-all-men; something set in opposition to all the wild beasts and demons that killed and afflicted men by day and night.

"Suppose there was a band of stone-people around here," suggested another man. People looked over their shoulders apprehensively. "They would be dangerous enemies to have, but strong friends."

The idea did not strike root: neither friendship nor enmity

with other bands had much importance in The People's life.

But Dart piped up: "This one wants to be our friend."

The oldest woman scoffed. "So would anyone who was crippled and needed help. Do you think he fought the lion just for your benefit?"

"Yes!"

A girl linguist's voice joined the muted hive that was buzzing anew in Derron's helmet. She provided him with a rather halting translation of part of the debate among The People, though after only a couple of minutes she was ordered away to work with another operator. From Operations voices in the background Derron overheard that so far two berserkers had been destroyed, but ten slave-units had been lost. And the appearance of the slave-units tended to terrify and scatter the people they were supposed to be protecting.

"Tell them to try pretending they're crippled," Derron advised. "All right, I'll do without a linguist if I have to. That may be better than getting a word or two wrong somewhere. But how about dropping me some of those self-defence weapons to hand out to these people? It'll be too late for that when the berserker comes back." The machine he had fought must have got sidetracked following some old trail, or pursuing some other band, but he had to assume that it would be back. "And drop me grenades, not arrows. There's only one man in this band who has a bow."

"The self-defence weapons are being prepared," someone assured him. "It's dangerous to hand 'em out until they're absolutely needed, though. Suppose they decide to use 'em on the slave? Or blow each other up by mistake?"

"I think it'll be more dangerous to wait too long. You can at least drop them now." Inside the slave's big torso was a chamber into which small items could be sent from the future as required.

"They're being prepared."

Derron didn't know whether he could believe that or not, the way things were going today.

The People seemed still to be discussing the slave-unit, while he kept it sitting in what he hoped was a patient and trustworthy attitude. According to the brief translation Derron had heard, the tall young man with the bow slung over his shoulder was the one arguing in favour of helping the "stone-man".

At last this man with the bow, who seemed to be the nearest thing to a chief that these people had, succeeded in talking one of the other men into helping him. Together they approached one of the saplings that had been splintered in the fight, and twisted it loose from its stump, hacking through the tough bark-strings with a hand axe. Then the two bold men brought the sapling right up to the edge of the poison-digger's trap. Gripping it by the branches, they pushed the splintered end down to where the slave could grasp it. Derron caught hold with both hands.

The two men pulled, then grunted with surprise at the weight they felt. The boy who had been up in the tree came to help.

"Odegard, this is Colonel Borss," said a helmet-voice in urgent tones. "We can see now what the berserkers' target is—the first written language on the planet originates very near your present location. The deaths so far haven't weakened its probability too much but of course one more killing could be the one to push it under the real-time threshold. There's a peduncle effect of course and we can't pinpoint the inventor, but the people in your band are certainly among the ancestors of his tribe."

Derron was clinging to the sapling as the slave-unit was dragged out over the edge of the pit. "Thanks for the word, colonel. How about those grenades I requested?"

"We're rushing two more slave-units into your sector there, Odegard, but we're having some technical troubles with them. Three of the enemy have been destroyed now ... grenades, you say?" There was a brief pause. "They tell me some grenades are coming up." The colonel's voice clicked off.

Their rescue job complete, The People had all fallen back a few steps, and were watching the machine carefully. Derron braced himself on one arm and repeated his peaceful gestures with the other. This seemed to reassure his audience about the slave, but they promptly found something else to worry about —the setting sun, which they kept glancing over their shoulders at as they talked to one another. Derron needed no linguist to know they were concerned about finding some place of relative safety in which to spend the night.

In another minute The People had gathered up their few belongings and were on the march, with the air of folk resuming a practiced activity. The man with the bow spoke several times to the slave-unit, and looked disappointed when his words were not understood, but he could not dally. Stone-man was left free to help himself as best he might.

So Derron trailed along at the end of The People's hiking file. He soon found that on level ground he could keep the slave-unit moving along pretty well on its long arms, walking it like a broken-backed ape on the knuckles of its hands with its legs dragging. The People cast frequent backward glances at this pathetic creature, regarding it with mixed and not altogether favourable emotions. But even more frequently they looked back farther in the direction they had come from, plainly fearful that something else could be on their trail.

If The People were not expecting the berserker machine, Derron was. The slave's leg-dragging track was certainly plain enough, and the sight of it might cause the killing machine to approach with some caution, but it would still come on.

Colonel Borss came back to talk the situation over. "Odegard, our screens show the berserker's area of disturbance moving south away from you and then coming back; evidently you were right about it being on a false trail of some kind. Your berserker is the only one we haven't bagged yet, but it seems to be in the most vital spot. What I think we'll do is this: the two slave-units being sent to reinforce you are going to catch up with your band in a few minutes present-time. We'll have them follow your band's line of march, keeping just out of sight, one on each flank; don't want to scare your people with a lot of metal-men, and have them scatter—we've had enough of that problem today. When your people stop somewhere for the night, you stay with 'em and we'll set the other two units up in ambush."

"Understand." Derron kept on walking with his arms, the master-unit rising and falling slightly with the bumpy terrain the slave was jolting over. A certain amount of feedback was necessary to give the operator the feeling of presence in the past.

The colonel's plan sounded reasonable, as Derron thought it over. And by Derron's interpretation of the law of averages, something should go right pretty soon.

Falling dusk washed the wilderness in a kind of dark beauty.

The People were marching with the swampy, half-wooded valley on their right and the low rocky hills now immediately on their left. The man with the bow, whose name seemed to be something like Matt, kept anxiously scanning these hills as he walked at the head of the file.

"What about dropping those grenades to me now? Ho, Operations? Anybody there?"

"We're setting up this ambush now, Odegard. We don't want your people hurling grenades around at random in the dark."

There was some sense in that, Derron supposed. And his slave could not throw anything efficiently while it had to walk and balance on its hands.

The leader Matt turned suddenly aside and went trotting up a barren hillside, the other people followed briskly. Scrambling after them as best he could, Derron saw that they were heading for a narrow cave entrance, set into a steep low cliff like a door into the wall of a house. Everyone halted a little distance away from the hole. Before Derron had quite caught up, Matt had unslung his bow and nocked an arrow. Another man then pitched a sizable rock into the darkness of the cave, having to stretch around an L-bend at the entrance to do so. At once there reverberated out of the depths a growl which scattered The People like the good survival experts they were.

When the cave-bear came to answer the door, it discovered the slave alone, a crippling foundling on the porch.

The bear's slap of greeting bowled the unbalanceable slave over. From a supine position Derron slapped back, bending the bear's snout slightly and provoking a blood-freezing roar. Made of tougher stuff than poison-diggers, the bear strained its fangs on the slave-unit's face. Still flat on his back, Derron lifted the bear with his steel arms and pitched it downhill. Go away!

The first roar had been only a tune-up for the one that followed. Derron didn't want to break even an animal's life-line here if he could help it, but time was passing and his real enemy would be drawing near. He threw the bear a little further this time. The animal bounced once, landed on its feet and running, and kept right on going into the swamp. Howls trailed in the air behind it for half a minute.

The People emerged from behind rocks and inside crevices and gathered slowly around the slave-unit, for once forgetting to look over their shoulders along the way they had come. Derron had the feeling that in another moment they were going to fall down and worship him; before any such business could get started he knuckle-walked the slave-unit into the cave and scanned the darkness—the slave's eyes adjusted quickly to see in whatever wave-lengths were present—to make sure it was unoccupied. It was a high narrow cavern with a second little window-like opening high up on the wall toward the rear. There was plenty of room to shelter the entire band; Matt had made a good discovery.

When he came out of the cave he found The People getting ready to build a good-sized fire at the mouth; they were gathering wood from under the trees at the edge of the swamp and lugging it hurriedly uphill. Far across the valley a small spark of orange burned in the thickening purplish haze of falling night, marking the encampment of some other band.

"Operations, how are those ambush arrangements coming along?"

"The other two units are just taking up their positions. They have you in sight at the mouth of the cave."

"Good."

Let The People build their fire, then, and let the berserker be drawn by it. It would find the band as well protected as they would ever be.

From a pouch of some tough skin one of the old women produced a bundle of bark, which she unwrapped to reveal a smouldering centre. With incantations and a judicious use of woodchips, she soon had the watchfire blazing. Its upper tongues reached high and bright against the fast-dimming sky.

The band filed into the cave, the slave-unit last to enter, right after Matt. Just inside the L-bend of the entrance, Derron sat his proxy leaning against the wall, and relaxed his arms with a great sigh. He was ready for a rest. Servo-assists or not, he had had a lot of exercise.

He had no sooner relaxed a notch than the night outside erupted without warning into battle. There was the crackle and slam of laser flame, the clang and squeal and crunch of armoured bodies meeting. The People in the cave jumped as one person to their feet.

In the flickering reflections of laser-light Derron could see Matt with his bow ready, facing the entrance, while the other adults looked for rocks to throw. In the rear of the cave the boy Dart had scrambled up to a perch from which he could look out of the high small window. The laser-light was bright on his awed face.

And then the lights went out. The flashing and crashing outside ended as abruptly as it had begun. Silence and darkness stretched on, in a death-like numbness.

"Operations? Operations? What's going on outside? What happened?"

"Oh my God, Odegard!" The voice was too shaken for him to identify. "Scratch two slave-units. Odegard, that—that damned thing's reflexes are just too good——"

The watchfire came exploding suddenly into the cave, transformed by the kick of a steel-clawed foot into a hail of sparks and brands that bounced from the curving wall of stone just opposite the narrow entrance and became a thousand scattered dying eyes on the cave floor. The berserker would be trying to flush its game, to see if there was a second exit through which the humans could try to run. It must know that the crippled slave-unit was inside the cave, but by now the berserker's cold computer-brain must have learned contempt for all that the android slaves of Time Operations could do against it. For, once it was satisfied that there was no way for its prey to escape, it tried to walk right in. There came a heavy grating sound; the cave mouth had proved just a bit too narrow for the machine to enter.

"Odegard, we've got a dozen arrows ready to drop to your unit now. Shaped charges in the points, set to fire on contact."

"*Arrows?* I said grenades! I told you we've got only one bow here, and there's no room for——" In mid-sentence Derron realized that the high little window in the rear of the cave might make an excellent archery port. "Send us arrows, then. Send something, quick!"

"We're dropping the arrows now. Odegard, we have a relief operator standing by in another master-unit, so we can switch if you need relief."

"Never mind that. I'm used to working this broken-backed thing now and he isn't."

The berserker was raising a hellish racket, scraping and

44

hammering at the stubborn bulge of rock which was keeping it from its prey. When a signal in his helmet told Derron that the arrows had arrived, he lost no time in using the slave's hands to open the door of its metal bosom. With a bank of awed faces turned to watch in the gloom, the slave-unit reached into its own metal heart to pull out a dozen shafts, which it then held out to Matt.

From the manner of their appearance it was plain they could be no ordinary arrows, and in the present situation there could be no doubt what their purpose must be. Matt delayed only a moment, holding the weapons with reverence, to make a sort of bow to the slave; and then he dashed to the rear of the cave and scrambled up to the window.

That window-hole would have provided him with a fine safe spot to shoot from, had the enemy possessed no projective weapons. But since the enemy was laser-armed, it would be the slave-unit's job to draw fire on itself and keep the berserker as busy as possible.

Hoping devoutly that Matt was an excellent shot, Derron inched his crippled metal body up to the very corner of the L-bend. He could feel the berserker's blows jarring through the rock he leaned against; he thought that if he reached around the corner he could touch it. Derron waited, looking back into the cave; and when he saw Matt nock the first magic-arrow to his bow, he went out around the corner with as quick a movement as he could manage on his hands.

And he nearly fell on his face, for the berserker was out of reach, having just backed away to take a fresh run at the cave entrance. Of course it was quicker with its laser than Derron was with his. The slave's armour glowed, but still held, while Derron scrambled forward, firing back. If the berserker saw Matt in his window it ignored him, thinking arrows meant nothing.

The first one struck the monster on the shoulder of one foreleg, the wooden shaft spinning viciously away while the head vanished in a momentary little fireball. The explosion left a fist-sized hole.

The machine lurched off balance even as its laser flicked toward Matt, and the beam did no more than set fire to the bush atop the little cliff. Derron was still scrambling toward the berserker as best he could, holding his own laser on it like

45

a spotlight, gouging the beam into the shoulder-wound. Matt popped up bravely and shot his second arrow as accurately as the first, hitting the berserker square in the side, so the punch of the shaped charge staggered it on its three legs. And then its laser was gone, for Derron had lurched close enough to swing a heavy metal fist and close up the projector-eye for good.

With that, the wrestling-match was on again. For a moment Derron thought that this time he had a chance, for the strength of the slave's two arms more than equalled that of the Berserker's one usable foreleg. But the enemy reflexes were still more than human. In a matter of seconds Derron was once more just hanging on, while the world spun. And then again he was thrown.

He grabbed at the legs that trampled him, trying to hang on somehow, to immobilize the berserker as a target. A stamping blow smashed his own laser. What was delaying the arrows?

The berserker was still too big, too strong, too quick, for the crippled slave to handle. Derron clung to one leg but the other two functional limbs kept on stomping like pile-drivers, tearing with their steel claws. There went one of the slave's useless feet, ripped clean off. The metal man was going to be pulled to pieces. *Where were the arrows?*

And then the arrows came. Derron had one glimpse of a hurtling human body above him, as Matt leaped directly into the fight, brandishing a cluster in each hand. Yelling, seeming to fly like some lightning-god of legend, he stabbed his bolts against the enemy's back.

Only a hint of lightning showed outside the berserker's body. The thunder was all deep inside, an explosion that bounced both machines. And with that, the fight was over.

Derron dragged the wrecked and overheated slave-unit shuddering out from under the mass of glowing, twisting, spitting metal that had been the enemy. Then, exhausted, he rested the slave on its elbows. In the wavering glow of the gutted berserker machine he saw Dart come running from the cave. Tears streaked the boy's face; in his hand was Matt's bow, the broken string dangling. And after Dart the rest of The People came running from the cave, to gather around something that lay motionless on the ground.

Derron made the slave sit up. Matt lay dead where the enemy's last convulsion had thrown him. His belly was torn

46

open, his hands charred, his face smashed out of shape—then the eyes opened in that ruined face. Matt's chest heaved for a shaky breath, and shuddered, and went on breathing.

The women wailed, and some of the men began a kind of slow song. Everyone made way as Derron crawled his battery proxy to Matt's side and lifted him as gently as he could. Matt was too far gone to wince at a few more minor burns from the slave's hot metal.

"Good work, Odegard." Colonel Borss's voice had regained strength. "Good work, you've wrapped the operation up. Can we drop you something to give that fellow some first aid?"

Derron bit back his first reply; maybe the colonel really hadn't seen. "He's in too bad shape for that, sir. You'll have to lift him with me."

"Would like to help, of course, but I'm afraid that's not in the regulations. . . ." The colonel's voice faded in hesitation.

"His lifeline is breaking here, colonel, no matter what we do. He won it for us, and now his guts are hanging out, Sir."

"Um. All right, all right. Stand by while we readjust for his mass."

The People were standing in an awed ring around the slave-unit and its dying burden. The scene would probably be assimilated into one of the historical myths, thought Derron. Perhaps the story of the dying hero and the stone-man would be found sometime amid some of the earliest writings of Sirgol. Myths were tough bottles, stretching to hold many kinds of wine.

Up at the mouth of the cave the oldest woman was having trouble with her tinder as she tried to get the watch-fire started again. A young girl who was helping grew impatient, and grabbed up a dried branch and ran down to the glowing berserker-shell. From that heat she kindled her brand; waving the flame to keep it bright, she moved back up the hill in a kind of dance.

And then Derron was sitting in a fading circle of light on the dark floor of Operations Stage Three. Two men were running toward him with a stretcher. He opened his metal arms to let the medics take Matt, and then turned his head inside his helmet and found the master power switch with his teeth.

He let the end-of-mission checklist go hang. In a matter of

seconds he had extricated himself from the master-unit, and was pushing his way past the first people coming toward him with congratulations. In his sweated leotard he hurried downstairs from the catwalk, and made his way through the throng of technicians, operators, medics and miscellaneous celebrants who were already crowding the floor of the stage. He reached Matt just as the medics were raising the stretcher with him on it. Wet cloths had been draped over the wounded man's protruding intestines, and an intravenous had already been started.

Matt's eyes were open, though of course they were stupid with shock. To Matt, Derron could be no more than another strange being among many; but Derron was one who walked beside him in human contact, gripping his forearm above his burned hand, until consciousness faded away.

As the stretcher moved toward the hospital it gathered with it something like a procession. As if a public announcement had been broadcast ahead, the word was spreading that for the first time a man had been brought up from the deep past. When they brought Matt into the emergency room it was only natural that Lisa, like everyone else in the hospital who had the chance, should come hurrying to see him.

"He's lost," she murmured, looking down at the swollen face, in which the eyelids now and then flicked open. "Oh, so lost and alone. I know the feeling." She turned anxiously to a doctor. "He'll live now, won't he? He's going to be all right?"

The doctor smiled faintly. "If they're breathing when we get 'em this far we usually save 'em."

Trusting Lisa sighed in immediate deep relief. Of course her concern for the stranger was natural and kind.

"Hello, Derron." She smiled at him briefly, before going to hover over the stretcher as closely as she could. Her voice and manner had been absent, as if she hardly noticed him at all.

48

PART TWO

His arms upraised, his grey beard and black robes whipping in the wind, Nomis stood tall on a table-top of black rock twenty feet square, a good hundred feet above the smashing surf. White seabirds coasted downwind toward him, then wheeled away with sharp little cries, like those of tiny souls in pain. Around his perch on three sides there towered other splintered crags and fingers of this coastline of black basaltic rock, while before him spread the immense vibration of the sea.

Feet braced apart, he stood centred in an intricate chalk diagram drawn on the flat rock. Around him he had spread the paraphernalia of his craft—things dead and dried, things old and carven, things that men of common thought would have deemed better destroyed and forgotten. In his thin penetrating voice Nomis was singing into the wind:

> "Gather, storm-clouds, day and night
> Lightning chew and water drown!
> Waves come swallowing, green and bright
> Chew and swallow and gulp it down—
> The craft in which my foe abides
> The long-ship that my enemy rides!"

There was much more to the song, and it repeated itself over and over. Nomis's thin arms quivered, tired from holding splinters of wrecked ships over his head, while the birds cried at him and the wind blew his thin grey beard up into his eyes.

Today he was weary, unable to escape the feeling that his day's labour was in vain. Today he had been granted none of the tokens of success that all too rarely came to him—heated symbol-dreams in sleep, or when awake, dark momentary

49

trances shot through with strange visions, startling stretchings of the mind.

Not often in his career had Nomis been convinced of his own power to call down evil on his enemies' heads. Success for him in this was a far more uncertain thing than he let others believe. Not that he doubted for a moment that the basic powers of the world were accessible through magic; it was only that success in this line seemed to call not only for great skill but for something like great good luck as well.

Twice before in his life Nomis had tried to raise a storm. Only once had he been successful, and the persistent suspicion remained that on that occasion the storm might have come anyway. At the height of the gale there had persisted a shade of doubt, a feeling that the ordering of such forces was beyond his powers or those of any man.

Now, doubtful as he was of present success, he persisted in the effort that had kept him almost sleepless on this secret rock for the past three days. Such was the fear and hatred he felt for the man he knew must now be crossing the sea toward him, coming with a new god and new advisers to assume the rule of this country called Queensland.

Nomis's grim eyes, turned far out to sea, marked there the passage of a squall-line, mockingly small and thin. Of the ship-killing tempest he worked to raise, there was no sign at all.

The cliffs of Queensland were still a day's rowing out of sight, dead ahead. In the same direction, but closer, some mildly bad weather was brewing. Harl frowned across the sea's grey face at the line of squalls, while his hands rested with idle sureness on the long-ship's steering-oar.

The thirty rowers, freemen and warriors all, could by simply turning their heads see the bad weather as easily as Harl could. And they were all experienced enough to reach the same conclusion, namely that by just slowing down the stroke a bit they would probably miss the squalls' path and so make themselves a bit more comfortable. So now by unspoken agreement they were all easing up a trifle on the oars.

From ahead a cool light breeze sprang up, fluttering the pennons on the sailless masts, and rippling the fringe of awning on the tent of royal purple which stood amidships.

Inside that tent, alone for the moment with his thoughts, was the young man that Harl called king and lord. Harl's frown faded as it crossed his mind that young Ay had probably withdrawn into the tent to make some plans for the fighting that was sure to come. The border tribes who cared nothing for the mild new god or the failing old Empire were certain to make some test of the will and courage of Queensland's new ruler—not that there were grounds for doubting the firmness of either.

Harl smiled at this next thought, that his young lord in the tent might not be planning war at all, but a campaign to make sure of the Princess Alix. It was her hand in marriage that was to bring Ay his kingdom and his army. All princesses were described as beautiful, but rumour said that this one also had spirit. Now if she was like some of the high-born girls that Harl had met, her conquest might be as difficult as that of a barbarian chieftain—and of course even more to a sturdy warrior's taste!

Harl's expression, which had become about as jovial as his facial scars would allow, faded once more to glumness. It had occurred to him that his king might have gone into the tent to practise reading. Ay had long been an admirer of books, and was actually bringing two of them with him on this voyage. Or it might be that he was praying to his gentle new slave-god, for young and healthy though he was, Ay now and then took the business of worship seriously.

Even while half his mind busied itself with these reflections, Harl of course remained alert as always. Now a faint puzzling splashing in the sea nearby caused him to turn his head to portside—and in a moment all the thoughts in his head were frozen, together with his warrior's blood.

Rearing right beside the ship, lifting its bulk across the horizon and the distant afternoon clouds, came a head out of nightmare, a dragon-face from some evil legend. The dully gleaming neck that bore the head was of a size that a man might just be able to encircle with both arms. Sea-demons alone might know what the body in the water below was like! the eyes were clouded suns, the size of silver platters, while the scales of head and neck were grey and heavy like thick wet iron. The mouth was a coffin, lid opened just a crack, all fenced inside with daggers.

Long as a cable, the thick neck came reeling inboard, scales rasping wood from the gunwale. The men's first cries were sounds such as warriors should not make, but in the next instant they were all grabbing bravely enough for their weapons. Big Torla, strongest of the crew, for once was quickest also, bracing a leg on his rower's bench and hacking with his sword at that tremendous swaying neck.

The blows clanged uselessly on dully gleaming scales; the dragon might not even have been aware of them. Its head swayed to a stop facing the doorway of the purple tent; from the slit of its terrible mouth there shrieked a challenge whose like Harl had not heard in a lifetime of war.

With all the clamour of voices and blows, Ay had needed no such summons to make ready. Before the dragon-bellow had ceased, the tent flaps were ripped open from inside and the young king stepped forth armed with shield and helm, sword ready in his hand.

Harl felt a tremendous pride to see that the young man did not flinch a hand's-breadth from the sight that met him. And with the pride Harl's own right arm came back to life, drawing from his belt his short-handled iron-bladed axe, and gripping it for a throw.

The axe clanged harmlessly from the clouded silver of one eye, perhaps not even felt. The dragon's enormous head, coffin-mouth suddenly gaping wide, lunged forward for the king.

Ay met it bravely. But the full thrust of his long sword, aimed straight into the darkness of the throat, meant no more than a jab from a woman's pin. The doorlike jaw slammed shut, crushing Ay instantly. For a moment, as the monstrous head swept away on its long neck, there was the horrible display of broken limbs dangling outside the teeth. And then, with one more faint splash beside the ship, the evil miracle was gone. The sunlit sea rolled on unchanged, its secrets all below.

Through the remaining hours of daylight, there was scarcely a word spoken aboard the long-ship. She prowled in watery circles, on and on, never getting far from the unmarked spot where her lord had been taken. She prowled in full battle-readiness, but there was not a thing for her to fight. The edge of the squall-line came, the men took mechanical measures to meet it. And the squall departed again, without the men ever having been really aware of its passage.

By the end of the day, the sea was calm again. Squinting into the setting sun, Harl rasped out a one-word order: "Rest."

Long ago he had retrieved his blunted axe and replaced it in his belt. Now the evidence to be seen on deck was only this: A few bits of wood, rasped from a raw scar on the gunwale, by scales hard as metal. A few small spots of blood. And Ay's winged helmet, fallen from his head.

Derron Odegard, recently decorated and promoted three grades to major, was sitting in as a junior aide on an emergency staff meeting called by the new Time Operations Commander. At the moment Derron was listening with both professional and friendly interest as his old classmate, Chan Amling, now a major in Historical Research, delivered an information briefing.

"...as we all know by now, the berserkers have chosen to focus this latest attack upon one individual. Their target, King Ay of Queensland, is naturally a man whose removal from history would have disastrous consequences for us.

Amling, quick-witted and fluent, smiled benignly over the heads of his audience. "Until quite recently most historians even doubted this man's reality. But of course since we have begun some direct observation of the past, his historicity and importance have both been fully confirmed."

Amling turned to an electric map, which he attacked with a teacher's gestures. "We see here the middle stages in the shrinkage and disorganization of the great Continental Empire, leading to its ultimate collapse. Now note Queensland here. It's very largely due to King Ay's activity and influence that Queensland can remain in such a comparatively stable state, preserving a segment of the Empire culture for our planet's later civilizations to base themselves on."

The new Time Operations Commander—his predecessor was reported to be now with a scouting expedition to the moon, or at least to Sirgol's surface, with Colonel Borss and others—raised a hand, student-like. "Major, I admit I'm not too clear on this. Ay was a bit of a barbarian himself, wasn't he?"

"Well, he certainly began as such, sir. But—oversimplifying somewhat—we can say that when he found himself with a land

53

of his own to defend, he settled down and defended it very well. Gave up his sea-roving ways. He had been one of the raiders and barbarians long enough to know all the tricks of that game. And he played it so well from the other side of the board that they usually preferred to attack someone else."

No one else had a question for Amling at the moment, and he sat down. The next officer to appear at the head of the table was a major from Probability Analysis, whose manner was no more reassuring than his information.

"Gentlemen," he began in a nervous voice, "we don't know how Ay was killed, but we do know where." The major displayed a videotape made from a sentry screen. "His lifeline is newly broken *here*, on his first voyage to Queensland. As you can see, all the other lifelines aboard ship remain unbroken. Probably the enemy expects historical damage to be intensified if Ay's own crew are thought to have done away with him. It seems to us in Probability that such an expectation is all too likely to be correct."

Amling looked as if he wanted to break in and argue; or, more likely, to make a wager on the subject. They had put Amling in the wrong section, Derron thought. Probability would have been the one for him.

The Probability major had paused for a sip of water. "Frankly, the situation looks extremely grave. In nineteen or twenty days' present-time the historical shockwave of Ay's assassination should reach us. That's all the time we have. I'm told that the chances of our finding the enemy keyhole within nineteen days are not good."

Edgy gloom was contagious, and the faces around the table were tightening in spite of themselves. Only the new Time Ops Commander managed to remain relatively relaxed. "I'm afraid you're right about the difficulty in finding this keyhole, major. Of course every effort is being made in that direction. Trouble is, the enemy's getting smart about hiding his tracks. This time he attacked with only one machine instead of six, which makes our job difficult to start with. And immediately after doing its job of assassination that one machine seems to have gone into hiding. It hasn't left Ay's time, it'll still be on the scene to mess up whatever we do to set things right, but meanwhile it's being careful not to cause any changes that we might use to track it."

Time Ops leaned forward, becoming less relaxed. "Now, who's got some ideas regarding countermeasures?"

The first suggestions involved trying to build Probability in Ay's later lifeline, so he would somehow have survived the assassination after all. This idea soon started an argument on a high technical level. In this the scientific people present of course dominated, but they were far from agreeing among themselves on what could and should be done. When they began to exchange personalities along with formulae, Time Ops called quickly for half an hour's recess.

Finding that much time unexpectedly on his hands, Derron stepped out and called the nurses' quarters at the nearby hospital complex. Lisa was living there now, while she started to train for some kind of nursing job. He was pleased to be able to reach her, and to hear that she too had some time to spare. Within a few minutes they were walking together, in the park where they had met for the first time.

Derron had come to the meeting with a topic of conversation all prepared, but Lisa these days was developing a favourite subject of her own.

"You know, Matt's just healing so quickly that all the doctors are amazed at it."

"Good. I'll have to come round and see him one of these days. I keep meaning to, but then I think I'll wait until we can talk to each other."

"Oh, goodness, he's talking now!"

"In our language? Already?"

She was delighted to confirm it, and elaborate. "It's like his rapid healing; the doctors say it must be because he comes from so far in the past. They talk about the effect on one individual of coming up through twenty thousand years' evolutionary gradient, about the organizational energies in his body and brain becoming infolded and intensified. I can't follow most of it, of course. They talk about the realm where the material and the non-material meet——"

"Yes."

"—and Matt probably understands what they're saying as well as I do now, if not better. He's up and around most of the time. They allow him a good deal of freedom. He's quite good about staying out of rooms he's warned not to enter, not touching dangerous things, and so forth."

55

"Yes."

"Oh, and did I tell you they've suspended healing in his face? Until they're sure he can make a fully informed decision on what he wants his new face to look like."

"Yes, I heard something about that. Lisa, how long are you going on living in the hospital? Are you really set on learning nursing, or is it just—something to do?" He almost asked, is it just Matt?

"Oh." Her face fell slightly. "Sometimes I don't think I was cut out to be a nurse. But I have no immediate plans to move. It's handy for me to live right in the hospital when I still get therapy for my memory every day."

"Any success with the treatments?" Derron knew that the doctors now fully accepted that Lisa had simply lost her memory through being caught in the path of the berserker missile. For a while some had considered it possible that she was an emissary or deserter from the future, made amnesic by descent through time. But on the sentry screens no such reversed lifeline could be found. In fact no traveller, no device, no message, had ever come from the future to this embattled civilization that called itself Modern. Possibly the inhabitants of the unknowable time-to-come had good reason of their own to refrain from communication; possibly the future Sirgol was not inhabited by man. Or it might simply be that this time of the berserker-war was completely blocked off from the future by paradox-loops. It was some comfort at least that no berserker machines came attacking from the direction of tomorrow.

"No, the therapy doesn't really help." Lisa sighed faintly; her memory of her personal life before the missile-wave caught her was still almost completely blank. She put the subject aside with a wave of her hand and went back to talking about what new things Matt had done today.

Derron, not listening, closed his eyes for a moment, savouring the sensation of life he had when he was with Lisa. At this moment he possessed the touch of her hand in his, the feel of grass and soil under his feet, the warmth of the pseudo-sunshine on his face. Next moment it might all be gone—another missile-wave could come down through the miles of rock, or the unravelling of King Ay's severed cord of life might propagate faster than expected up through the fabric of history.

He opened his eyes and saw the muralled walls surrounding the buried park, and the improbably alive, singing and soaring birds. Down here at the level where humans walked the place was almost thronged, as usual, with strolling couples and solitaries; in places the tough grass was showing signs of wear, and the gardeners had had to defend it with string fences. All in all, a poor imitation of the murdered real world; but with Lisa beside him it became transformed into something better than it was.

Derron pointed. "Right there's the tree where I first came to your rescue. Or you came to mine, rather."

"*I* rescued *you*? From what horrible fate?"

"From dying of loneliness in the midst of forty million people. Lisa, I'm trying to tell you that I want you to move out of that hospital dormitory."

Her eyes turned away, looking down. "If I did that, where would I live?"

"I'm asking you to live with me, of course. You're not a little lost girl any more, you're on your own, studying to be a nurse, and I can ask. There are some unused apartments around, and I'll rate one of them if I take a companion. Especially with this promotion they've given me."

She squeezed his hand, but that was all. She was thoughtfully silent, her eyes on the ground a few paces ahead of them.

"Lisa? What do you say?"

"Just *exactly* what are you offering me, Derron?"

"Look, yesterday when you were telling me about your new girl friends' problems you seemed to have a very firm grasp of what this male-female business is all about."

"You want me to live with you temporarily, is that it?" Her voice was cool and withdrawn.

"Lisa, nothing in our world can be permanent. At the staff meeting just now—well, I'm not supposed to talk about that. But things don't look good. I want to share with you whatever good things may be left."

Still silent, she let him lead her on stepping-stones across the park's little stream.

"Lisa, do you want a marriage ceremony? I should have put that first, I suppose, and asked you formally to marry me. The thing is, not many people are going to raise their eyebrows if

57

we do without a ceremony, and if we do without one we'll avoid some delay and red tape. Would you think we were doing wrong if we didn't have a wedding?"

"I . . . suppose not. What bothers me is the way you talk about everything being temporary. I suppose feelings are included."

"When everything else is temporary, yes! That doesn't mean I necessarily like it. But how can anyone in our world say what they'll be feeling or thinking a month or a year from now? In a year we'll most likely all . . ." He let his voice trail off.

She had been searching for words, and now at last she found the ones she wanted. "Derron, at the hospital I've absorbed the attitude that people's lives can be made less temporary, now or any time. That people should go on trying to build, to accomplish things, even though they may not have long to live."

"You absorbed this at the hospital, you say?"

"All right, maybe I've always felt that way."

He had, too, at one time. A year, a year and a half ago. A lifetime ago, with someone else. The image that he could not stop seeing and did not want to stop seeing came back to him again.

Lisa seemed to have her own private image. "Look at Matt, for instance. Remember how badly hurt he was. Look at what an effort of will he's made to survive, and recover——"

"I'm sorry," Derron interrupted, looking at the time, finding valid excuse for getting away. "I've got to run. I'm almost late at the staff meeting."

The scientists, by some combination of calculation and debate, had reached a consensus.

"It comes down to this," their newly-elected spokesman explained, when the staff meeting had resumed. "If we're to have any hope of healing the break in Ay's lifeline we must first immobilize the affected part, to minimize damage—something like putting a splint on a broken arm or leg."

"And just how do we go about splinting a lifeline?" demanded Time Ops.

The scientist gestured wearily. "Commander, the only way I can suggest is that someone be sent to take Ay's place temporarily. To continue his interrupted voyage to Queensland, and there play his part for a few days at least. The man sent could carry a communicator with him, and be given day-to-day or even hour-to-hour instructions from here, if need be. If the berserkers stood still for it, he might play out the remainder of Ay's life in its essentials, well enough to let us survive."

"How long do you think any man could play a part like that successfully?" someone broke in.

"I don't know." The scientists' spokesman smiled faintly. "Gentlemen, I don't know if a substitution scheme can be made to work at all. Nothing like it has ever been tried. But I think it will at least buy us a few more days or weeks of present-time in which to think of something else."

Time Ops thoughtfully rubbed his stubbled face. "Well now, substitution is the only idea we've got to work with at this point. But Ay is about twelve hundred years back. That means that dropping a man from here to take his place is out of the question. Right?"

"Afraid so, sir," said a biophysicist. "Mental devolution and serious memory loss sets in at about four hundred years."

Time Ops thought aloud in a tired monotonous voice. "Does anyone suppose we could get away with using a slave-unit on this kind of job? No, I thought not. They just can't be made convincingly human enough. Then what's left? We must use one of Ay's contemporaries. Find a man who's able to do the job, motivate him to do it, and then train him."

Someone suggested: "Appearance isn't too much of a problem. Ay isn't known in Queensland, except by reputation, when he first arrives there."

Colonel Lukas, the Psych Officer on Time Ops' staff, cleared his throat and spoke. "We ought to be able to get Ay's crew to accept a substitute, provided they *want* Ay to be alive, and if we can snatch the whole bunch of them up to present-time for a few days' work."

"We can manage that if we have to," Time Ops said.

"Good." Lukas doodled thoughtfully on a pad before him. "Some tranquillizer and pacifier drugs would be indicated first ...then we can find out whatever details of the assassination we need to know... then a few days' hypnosis. I'm sure we can work something out."

"Good thinking, Luke." Time Ops looked round the table. "Now, gentlemen, before it should slip our minds, let's try to solve the first problem, the big one. Who is our Ay-substitute going to be?"

Surely, thought Derron, someone besides me must see where one possible answer lies. He didn't want to be the first one to suggest it, because . . . well, just because. No! Hellfire and damnation, why shouldn't he? He was being paid to think, and he could put forward this thought with the clearest conscience in the world. He cleared his throat, startling men who seemed to have forgotten his presence.

"Correct me if I'm wrong, gentlemen. But don't we have one man available now who might be sent down to Ay's century without losing his wits? I mean the man who comes from the even deeper past himself."

Harl's duty was painfully clear in his own mind. He was going to have to take the ship on to Queensland, and when he got there he was going to have to stand before King Gorboduc and the princess, look them in the face and tell them what had happened to Ay. Harl was gradually realizing already that his story might not be believed. And what then?

The rest of the crew were spared at least the sudden new weight of responsibility. Now, many hours after the monster's attack, they were still obeying Harl without question. The sun was going down, but Harl had started them rowing again, and he meant to keep them rowing for Queensland right through the night, to hold off the mad demonstration of grief that was sure to come if he let the men fall idle now.

They were rowing now like blind men, sick men, walking dead men, their faces blank with rage and shock turned inward, neither knowing nor caring where the ship was steered. Frequently the oars fell out of stroke, clattering together or splashing awkwardly along the surface of the sea. No one quarrelled at this, or even seemed to notice. Torla groaned a death-song as he pulled—woe to the next man who faced Torla in a fight.

Inside the purple tent, atop the chest that held Ay's personal treasure (that chest was another problem for Harl, a problem that would grow as rage and grief wore away), the winged helmet now rested in a place of honour. It was now all that was left . . .

Ten years ago Ay had been a real prince, with a real king for a father. At about that time Ay's beard had first begun to sprout, and Harl had first begun to serve as the young prince's good right hand. And at about that time, also, the twin sicknesses of envy and treachery had started to spread like the plague among Ay's brothers and uncles and cousins. Ay's father and most of his house had died in that plague, and the kingdom had died too, being lost and divided among strangers.

Ay's inheritance had shrunk to the deck of a fighting ship—not that Harl had any objection to that on his own account. Harl had not even complained about books and reading. Nor even about prayers to a man-god, a slave-god who had preached love and mercy and had gotten his bones split with wedges for his trouble ...

Over the ship, or beneath it, there suddenly passed a force, a tilting, swaying motion, over in an instant. Harl's first thought was that the dragon had come back, rising from the deep to scrape its bulk beneath the long-ship's hull. The men evidently thought the same, for in an instant they had dropped their oars and drawn their weapons again.

But there was no dragon to be seen, nor much of anything else. With a speed that seemed nothing short of supernatural, a mist had closed in round the ship; the red lingering light of sunset had been transformed into a diffused white glow. Looking round him now, battle-axe ready in his hand, Harl noticed that even the rhythm of the waves was different. The air was warmer, the very smell of the sea had changed.

The men looked wild-eyed at one another in the strange soft light. They fingered their swords and muttered about wizardry.

"Row slowly ahead!" ordered Harl, putting the useless axe back in his belt. He tried to sound as if he had some purpose other than keeping the men busy, though in fact his sense of direction had for once been totally confused.

He gave the steering oar to Torla, and went forward himself to be lookout. Then before the rowers had taken fifty slow strokes he threw up a hand to halt them, and water gurgled round the backing oars. No more than an easy spear-cast from the bow, a gentle sandy beach had materialized out of the greyness. What manner of land might be behind the beach it was impossible to tell.

When the men saw the beach, their murmuring grew louder.

61

They knew full well that only a few minutes ago there had been no land of any kind in sight.

"Yet that's certainly solid ground ahead."

"*Looks* like solid ground. I'd not be surprised to see it vanish in a puff of smoke."

"Sorcery!"

Sorcery, certainly; no one disputed that. Some kind of magic, good or bad, was at work. What might be done about it, if anything, was another question. Harl quit pretending he knew what he was about, and called a council. After some debate it was decided that they should row straight away from the beach, to see if they might in that way get beyond the reach of whatever enchantment held them in its grip.

Sunset was now long overdue, but the pale light filtering down through the mist did not fade. In fact it became brighter, for as they rowed the mist began to thin.

Just as they emerged from the fog-bank, and Harl was beginning to hope they were indeed getting away from the enchantment, they came near driving their ship straight into a black, smooth, almost featureless wall that rose from the sea. The wall was slightly concave, and it had no edge or top in sight, it rose and extended and curved back without limit around the sea and over the mist. From the foot of this wall the men looked up to find it made an enormous inverted bowl over their tiny ship; from near the zenith, far above their heads, lights as bright and high as sun-fragments threw down their fire on white fog and black water.

Men cried out prayers to all the gods and demons known. Men shrieked that they had come to the sky and the stars at the end of the world. They almost broke their oars, pulling on them to spin their ship and drive it back into the mist.

Harl was as much shaken as any other, but he swore to himself to die before showing it. One man had collapsed to the deck, where he lay with hands over his eyes, groaning "Enchantment, enchantment!" over and over. Harl kicked and wrestled him viciously back to his feet, meanwhile seizing the idea and putting it to use.

"Aye, enchantment, that's all!" Harl shouted. "Not a real sky or stars, but something put into our eyes by magic. Well, if there be wizards here who mean us harm, I say they can be made to bleed and die like other men. If they are thinking to

62

have some fun with us, well, we know a game or two ourselves!"

The others took some heart from Harl's words. Back here in the concealing fog, the world was still sane enough so a man could look around at it without losing his powers of thought.

In an almost steady voice, Harl gave the order to row back in the direction of the beach they had glimpsed earlier. The men willingly obeyed; the man who had collapsed pulled hardest, looking to right and left at his fellows as if daring any to make some comment. But he would be safe from jokes, it seemed, for a good while yet.

They were not long in coming to the gentle sloping beach again; it proved to be real and solid. As the long-ship slid lightly aground, Harl, sword in hand, was the first to leap into the shallows. The water was warmer than he had expected, and when a splash touched his lips he discovered it was fresh. But by this time he was beyond being surprised at such relative trifles.

One of Matt's tutors stepped ahead of Derron, tapped on the door of the private hospital room, then slid it open. Putting his head inside, the tutor spoke slowly and distinctly: "Matt? There is a man here who wants to talk to you. He is Derron Odegard, the man who fought beside you in your own time."

The tutor turned to motion Derron forward. As he entered the room, the man who had been sitting in an armchair before the television screen got to his feet, standing tall and erect.

In this man, dressed in the robe and slippers that were general issue for hospital patients, Derron saw no resemblance to the dying savage he had helped a few days ago to carry into the hospital. Matt's hair had been depilated and was only now starting to grow back in, a neutral-coloured stubble. Matt's face below the eyes was covered by a plastic membrane, which served as skin while the completion of the healing process was held in abeyance.

On a bedside table, half-covered by some secondary-level schoolbooks, were several sketches and composite photographs, looking like variations on one basic model of a young man's face. Derron was now carrying in his pocket a photo of a somewhat different face—Ay's, caught by a spy device sent, in the shape of a bird, to skim near the young king-to-be on the day he began his fateful voyage to Queensland. That was the closest the Moderns had been able to get to the spacetime locus of the assassination—as usual, paradox-loops strongly resisted repeated interference with history at any one spot.

"I am pleased to meet you, Derron." Matt put genuine meaning into the ritual phrase. His voice was quite deep; at most, a little minor work would be needed to match it to Ay's, which had been recorded when the photo was made; Matt's manner of speaking, like his tutor's to him, was slow and distinct.

"I am pleased to see that your health is returning," Derron answered. "And glad that you are learning the ways of a new world so quickly."

"And I am pleased to see that you are healthy, Derron. I am glad your spirit could leave the metal-man it fought in, for that metal-man was very much hurt."

Derron smiled, and nodded toward the tutor, who had taken up a jailer's or servant's stance just inside the door. "Matt, don't let them con you with talk of where my spirit was. I was never in any direct danger, as you were, during that fight."

"Con me?" Matt had the question-inflection down pat.

The tutor said: "Derron means, don't let us teach you wrong things. He's joking."

Matt nodded impatiently, knowing about jokes. A point had been raised that was quite serious for him. "Derron, but it was your spirit in the metal-man?"

"Well—say it was my electronic presence."

Matt glanced at the television built into the wall. He had turned down the sound when company entered; some kind of historical documentary was being shown. He said: "Electronics I have learned a little bit. It moves my spirit from one place to another."

"Moves your eyes and thoughts, you mean."

Matt seemed to consider whether he was understanding the words correctly, and to decide that he was. "Eyes and thoughts and spirit," he said firmly.

The tutor said: "This spirit-orientation is really his idea, major, not something we've inculcated."

"I understand that," said Derron mildly. The important thing, from Operations' point of view, would be this tendency of Matt's toward firmness of opinion, even in a new world.

64

Such firmness would be a very good thing in an agent—provided the right opinions were held, of course.

Derron smiled. "All right, Matt. In the spirit I was fighting beside you, though I didn't risk my neck as you risked yours. When you jumped onto that berserker, I know your thought was to save me. I am grateful, and I am glad that now I can tell you so."

"Will you sit down?" Matt gestured Derron to a chair, then reseated himself; the tutor remained standing, hovering in the background.

Matt said: "My thought was partly to save you. Partly for my people there, partly just to see the berserker die. But since coming here I have learned that all people, even here, might be dead if we had not won that fight."

"That is true. But the danger is not over. Other fighting, just as important, is going on in other times and places." This was a suitable opening for the recruiting speech he had been sent here to make. But Derron paused before plunging ahead. For the tenth time he wished that Operations had sent someone else to do this job. But the experts thought Matt was most likely to react favourably if the representation was made by Derron, the man who had, in a sense at least, fought beside him. And using Matt was Derron's own idea, after all. Yes, he kept coming back to that in his thoughts. He hadn't seen Lisa since that last walk in the park—maybe he had been avoiding her. Yes, he could wish now that he had kept his mouth shut at the staff meeting.

Anyway, in the present situation, if Derron didn't make the sales pitch someone else would, perhaps less scrupulously. So he vented an inaudible sigh and got down to business. "Already you have done much for us, Matt. You have done much for everyone. But now my chiefs send me to ask if you are willing to do more."

He gave Matt the essence of the situation, in simplified form. The berserkers, deadly enemies of the tribe-of-all-men, had gravely wounded a great chief in another part of the world. It was necessary that someone should take the chief's place for a time.

Matt sat quietly, his eyes steadily attentive above the plastic skin that masked most of his face. When Derron had finished his preliminary outline of Operations' plan, Matt's first question was: "What will happen when the great chief is strong again?"

"Then he will resume his own place, and you will be brought back here to live in our world. We expect we will be able to bring you back safely—but you must understand that there will be danger. Just how much danger we cannot say, because this will be a new kind of thing for us to do. But there will certainly be some danger, all along the way."

Let him know that, major—don't paint too black a picture, of course. It seemed to be left up to Major Odegard to find the proper shade of grey. Well, Time Ops might be spying over his shoulder right now, but Derron was damned if he'd con Matt into taking a job that he, Derron, wouldn't have touched if it had been open to him. No, Derron told himself, *he* wouldn't volunteer if he could. What had the human race done for him lately? Really, the chances of the mission's doing anyone any good seemed to him very uncertain. Death did not frighten him any more, but there were things that still did—physical pain, for one. For another, the chance of meeting, on a mission like this, some unforeseeable ugly fate in the half-reality called probability-space, which the Moderns had learned to traverse but had hardly begun to understand.

"And if in spite of all medicine the great chief should die, and can never go back to his own place?"

"Then it would be your job to continue in his place. When you needed advice we would tell you what to do. In this king's place you would lead a better life than most men in history have had. And when you had finished out his span of years, we would try to bring you here to our world again, to live on still longer, with much honour."

"Honour?"

The tutor tried to explain.

Matt soon seemed to grasp what was meant, and went on to raise another point. "Would I take more magic-arrows with me, to fight the berserkers?"

Derron thought about it. "I suppose you might be given some such weapon, to protect yourself to some degree. But your main job would not be fighting berserkers directly, but acting for this king, as he would act, in other matters."

Matt nodded, as slowly and precisely as he spoke. "All is new, all is strange. I must think about it."

"Of course."

Derron was about to add that he could come back tomorrow for an answer, but Matt suddenly had two more questions. "What will happen if I say no? If no one can be found to take the place of the wounded chief?"

"There is no way that you, or anyone, can be forced to take his place. Our wise men think that if no one does, the war will be lost and all of us will probably be dead in less than a month."

"And I am the only one who can go?"

"It may be so. You are our wise men's first choice." An operation was now under way to recruit a back-up man or two from the deep past. But anyone else brought up now would remain days behind Matt all the way through the process of preparation, and every hour was deemed important.

Matt spread out his healed hands. "I must believe what you tell me, you who have saved my life and made me well again. I do not want to die in a month, and see everyone else die. So I must do what the wise men want, go and take this chief's place if I am able."

Derron puffed out his breath, venting mixed feelings. He reached into his pocket for the photo.

Time Ops, sitting in a small rough cavern a good distance from Operations, and watching through one of his system of secret scanners, nodded with satisfaction and mild surprise. That Odegard was a sharp young lad, all right. No outward display of gung-ho enthusiasm but always good work, including this job—a smooth soft sell that had gotten the volunteer to place himself on the right side of the question.

Now the operation could get rolling in earnest. Time ops swivelled in his chair and watched Colonel Lukas pull a white nightgown-like robe over his head and down, concealing the plastic chain-mail that guarded him from throat to knee.

"Luke, you've got some bare face and hands hanging out," Time Ops remarked, frowning. Psych Officers as good as Lukas were hard to find. "These boys you're going to meet are carrying real knives, you know."

Lukas knew. Swallowing, he said: "We haven't got time to be thinking up foolproof protective gimmicks. I won't inspire any confidence if I go out there looking like a masked demon, believe me."

Time Ops grunted and got up. He stood for a moment behind the radar operator to note the image of the ship on the beach, and the cluster of tiny green dots in front of her—her crew, come ashore. Then he went on to the window, a wide hole hacked crudely through a wall of rock, and squinted out from between the two heavy stun-projectors and their ready gunners. As the fog-generators outside were very near the window, there was nothing to be seen but billows of opaque whiteness, streaming out and away. Time Ops picked up and put on a set of heavy glasses like those the gunners were wearing. The fog effectively disappeared; now he could see the individual men standing before their ship a hundred yards away, and the great calm surface of the Reservoir beyond.

"All right," he said reluctantly. "I guess we'll be able to see you wave your arm—if they don't surround you and get in our way. If that happens, wave your arms over your head and we'll cut loose."

"I just don't want anyone to get trigger-happy, Commander," said Lukas, looking uneasily at the gunners. "We're going to have to do some very delicate work on those men out there, and that won't be easy and may not be possible if they've taken a hard stunning. I'd much rather ease them along with the drugs, and ask them some questions and make some impression on them along the way."

Time Ops shrugged. "It's your baby. Got your gas mask?"

"Yes. Remember, we'll try to do the job with the pacifier-tranquillizer mix in the drinks; they're physically tired and that may put 'em right to sleep. But don't hesitate to use the gas." Lukas took a last look around.

"Looks like a few of them are starting up from the beach," said the radar man.

Lukas jumped. "Here I go, then. Where're my servants? Ready? Tell them to keep inside at first. Here I go!" His sandalled feet thudded rapidly down a stair.

The sand beach sloped up to a lowland of gravelly soil and sparse grass of the kind that grew in shadow. Harl left the bulk of the crew at the water's edge, ready to protect the ship or shove her off again, while with six chosen men he proceeded slowly inland.

The scouting party had not far to go; they had scarcely passed over the first hillock before they saw a single tall figure come walking toward them through the mist. This figure drew close and became a man of impressive mien, dressed in a white robe such as the Good Enchanters of the old religions wore.

Showing not the least surprise or fear at being confronted by seven armed sea-rovers, this man came near to them and stopped, raising his hands in a gesture of peace. "My name is Lukas," he said simply. He spoke in Harl's native language— with a bad accent, but Harl in his travels had managed to understand worse.

"Let us put some pointed questions to this 'chanter," said Torla at once, setting a hand on his dagger.

The one in wizard's garb raised his eyebrows, and his right hand and wrist flexed up slightly from his side. Perhaps only a gesture of remonstrance, but perhaps giving or preparing to give a signal.

"Let us wait!" said Harl sharply. In this mist, a small army might lie concealed within spear-cast. Harl nodded to Lukas politely, and gave the names of himself and his companions.

The white-robed man, his hands once more innocently at rest, bowed in grave acknowledgement. He said: "My house is very near; allow me to offer you its hospitality, at least for a meal."

"We thank you for the offer," said Harl, not liking the uncertainty in his own voice. The man's air of confidence had an unsettling effect. Harl wanted to ask what country they had landed in, but was reluctant to reveal his ignorance.

"I pray you," Lukas asked, "some or all of you come to my house, at least for food and drink. If you wish to leave men to guard your ship, I will order some refreshment sent to them."

Harl mumbled for a moment, undecided. He tried to imagine how Ay would have met this strange confident courtesy. Lukas hardly needed powers of clairvoyance to know that seven sea-rovers newly arrived on his beach had come by ship; but he might have come scouting to find out just how many men and ships there were.

"Wait here for a moment," Harl answered at last. "Then we seven will go with you." Two men stayed with Lukas while

Harl and the others walked back over the little hill to explain matters to the rest of the crew. Some of these also argued for seizing the wizard at once and asking him pointed questions.

Harl shook his head. "We can do that at any moment. But enchanters are likely to be stubborn and prideful. And once a man's blood is out, it's hard to pour it back into his veins should the letting prove to have been a mistake. We'll just watch him close, until we learn more. If food and drink are sent you, I suggest you treat the bearers with some courtesy." He need give the men no urging to caution and alertness; they were ready to strike at shadows now.

So Harl and his chosen six ringed themselves about Lukas and walked inland with him. Taking their cue from Harl, the six other sea-rovers tried to look as if the encirclement was all accidental and unintentional, as if their hospitable host was not really their prisoner. And Lukas might have taken his cue from them, for he gave no sign of being bothered in the least.

As the party proceeded inland the mist grew thicker with each step. Before they had gone a hundred paces they found their way blocked by a line of low cliffs, hitherto invisible, from the top of which the greyness came rolling down. Built right against the foot of this cliff was the wizard's house; it was a simple stone building, with a look of newness, only one story high but big and solid enough to be a manor or a small fortress. At second glance, though, it was hardly a fortress, for the windows were low and wide, and the wide doorway stood unprotected by moat or wall.

Several people in simple servants' garb emerged from this doorway and bowed to the approaching Lukas and his guests; Harl noticed with some relief that none of the servants appeared to be anything more or less than human. The girls among them were comely, in a down-to-earth and lively style; they eyed the warriors sideways and giggled before popping back inside.

"No fairy-tale witches there," growled Torla. "Though I make no doubt they know enchantments of a sort."

Torla preceded Lukas through the doorway, with the rest of the sea-rovers then following close on the heels of the white-robed man. Harl was last to enter, looking behind him as he did so, his hand on his axe. He could not begin to feel easy about any man who welcomed seven armed strangers into his house.

Inside there was nothing to feed Harl's suspicions, save more of the same strange confidence. The entrance opened directly into a great manorial room, in which were set more than enough tables and benches to have accommodated the longship's entire crew. At the huge hearth, a smiling confident servant stood turning the spitted carcass of a weighty meat-animal. The roast was browned and dripping, so nearly done that it must have been started hours before.

Though a fair amount of light came in at the windows with the fog, the walls were mounted with enough torches to make the room quite bright. Through simple hangings which covered the rear wall, Harl could now and then glimpse servants going about tasks in distant chambers which must be dug back behind the line of the cliff. There was of course no way of telling how many armed men might be in those rooms, or lurking somewhere outside, but so far Harl had not seen a single weapon, barring table knives. Another easy-mannered servant was now laying out eight places at the head table, setting out worthy but not spectacular silver plates and tankards along with the cutlery.

Lukas proceeded straight to the head of the table—a couple of the sea-rovers keeping casually close to him—and turned with a gracious gesture. "Will you be seated? There is wine or ale, as you choose."

"Ale!" barked Harl, giving each of his men a meaningful look. He had heard of potent drugs and poisons whose taste blended very smoothly with that of wine; and even honest drink must not be allowed to take the edge of clearness from their minds. The others echoed Harl's call for ale, though Torla looked somewhat disappointed.

The company seated themselves, and two girls promptly came from behind the hangings to fill their tankards. Harl watched to see that the wizard's drink was poured from the same vessel as his own, and Harl waited until the wizard was wiping foam from his own lips before he tasted the drink himself. And even then Harl took only a sparing swallow.

The ale was neither too strong nor too weak, but ... yes, there was something slightly peculiar in its taste. Still, Harl asked himself, in a place where everything was strange, how

71

could the ale be otherwise? And he allowed himself another sip.

"The ale of your country is strong and good," he ventured then, stretching the truth to make a compliment. "So no doubt you have many strong men here, and serve a strong king."

Lukas bowed slightly. "All that you say is true."

"And your king's name?"

"Our present king is called the *Planetary Commander*." The wizard smacked his lips over ale. "And whom do you serve?"

A tremulous groan passed round the board. The tankards scraped in unison as they were lifted, and then together they thudded down, all lighter than they had been. All except Harl's. He had not observed the least sign of treachery—come to think of it, there was no reason why there should be any treachery—but still he decided firmly that he would not drink any more. Not just now.

"Who *do* we serve?" he asked the world. "Our good young lord is dead."

"Young Ay is dead!" Torla roared it out, like a man challenging the pain of some dreadful wound. A serving-girl came to refill his tankard, and Torla seized her and pulled her onto his lap. But when with her thin weak arms she resisted his pawing he only held her there gently, while a comical witless expression grew slowly on his face.

Something about this made Harl wonder. His own mind was perfectly clear . . . and yet he should be more concerned, more alert than he was. Should he not?

"Young Ay's death would be sad news," said Lukas calmly. "If it were true." The wizard seemed to be slumping slowly in his chair, utterly relaxed, forgetting dignity.

Oddly, no one took offence at the implication that they would be untruthful in such a matter. The men only sipped, or drank, and passed another murmur of mourning round the table.

"We saw him die!"

"Ah, yes!"

Harl's big fists were knotted, remembering their helplessness against the dragon. "We saw him die, in such a way that by all the gods I can scarce believe it yet myself!"

Lukas leaned forward, suddenly intent. "And what way was that?"

In a faltering voice Harl told him. Harl's throat quickly grew dry with speech; hardly realizing that he did so, he interrupted his tale to take another swallow from his tankard. The truth about the dragon sounded in his own ears like a clumsy lie. What chance was there of King Gorboduc believing it?

When Harl's recital was finished, Torla started to stand up as if he meant to speak. The girl fell from his lap and landed with a yelp on her soft bottom. Torla, his face showing uncharacteristic concern, bent as if to help her. But she scurried away, and Torla just kept right on bending until he was seated again, with his head lying on the table. Then he began to snore.

Torla's shipmates, those who were not on the verge of snoring themselves, only laughed at this. The men were all tired...no. Something *was* wrong, they should not be drunk on one or two tankards apiece of any ale. And if they were drunk, some of them at least should be quarrelsome. Harl puzzled over the strangeness of this, took another thoughtful sip himself, and decided he had better get to his feet.

"Your king is not dead," the wizard was telling him monotonously. "Not dead, not dead. Why should you believe that he is?"

"*Why?* We saw the—the dragon take him." But Harl was no longer quite sure of what he had seen or what he remembered. What was happening here? He swayed on his feet, half-drew his sword, and croaked: "Treachery! Wake up!"

His men's eyes were glassy, or closing, their faces foolish. Some of them started to rise at his cry, but then they sank back, leaning on the table, letting weapons slide forgotten to the floor.

"Wizard," one man muttered, turning pleading eyes toward Lukas. "Tell us again that our king lives."

"He lives and shall live."

"He—he is——" Harl could not make himself say that Ay was dead. In terror of he knew not what, he staggered back from the table, his sword sighing all the way out of its scabbard into his hand. To hurt anyone for any reason would be a monstrous crime, but he felt so frightened that he might do anything. "Stand back!" he warned the wizard.

The wizard also stood up, not frightened with the length of

the table between himself and Harl. From inside his robe Lukas took a mask like an animal's snout, which he fitted onto his face. His voice came out thickly: "No one will harm you here. I have shared with you the drink that makes men peaceful. Sit down now and talk with me."

Harl turned and ran for the door. Outside, the mist suddenly turned sparkling in his lungs. He ran on until he reached the hillock from which he could see the beached ship, only to discover that all the men he had left there were dead or dying. Half a dozen nearly-human monsters with grey snouted faces were busy arranging their bodies in rows on the beach. Those of his crew who could still move were offering no resistance, but were letting themselves be led like load-oxen.

It was really too bad that such a thing had happened. Harl groped reflexively for his sword and axe, and then remembered that he had thrown his weapons away somewhere.

"It's all right." Lukas's soothing voice came from just behind Harl. As Harl turned, the wizard continued: "Your men are all asleep. They need rest. Don't wake them."

"Ahh, that's it!" Harl sighed with relief. He might have known there was no reason to worry, not on this good island of sparkling ale and sparkling air and friendly people who spoke nothing but truth. He saw now that the snouted monsters were only men who wore masks like the wizard's. They were taking good care of his men. Harl looked confidently at Lukas, waiting to be told some more good news.

Lukas seemed to relax, sighing behind his mask. "Come here," he said. And he led Harl down to the water's very edge, where the wet sand was kept lapped to perfect smoothness by the little wavelets coming in.

With his finger the wizard drew in the wet sand, making the crude outline of a grotesque head. "Suppose now that this is the dragon you thought you saw. What exactly did you think happened?"

Harl groaned wearily and sank to his knees, staring helplessly at the sketch. Now that he could relax, he felt very tired, and soon he was going to sleep. But right now he had to concentrate on what the wizard was showing him. "It seized Ay," Harl said. "In its mouth."

"Like this?" The wizard's finger drew a stick-figure clenched in the dragon's teeth, waving helpless lines of arms and legs.

74

Even as he drew, the little waves were coming in over the sketch, smoothing and blurring its lines.

"Like that," Harl agreed. He sat down awkwardly.

"But now all that is being wiped out," the wizard intoned. "Wiped away. And when this evil thing is gone, then the truth, what you and I want to be the truth, can be written in, to fill its rightful place."

The waves were coming in, coming in, erasing the dragon. And Harl could sleep.

Somewhere along the line, during his hurried days of training, Matt asked: "Then King Ay is in fact dead, and not wounded, as I was first told?"

A tutor explained: "You were told he was only wounded, because he can be brought back to life. If your mission succeeds, his dying and his wounds will be as if they had never happened."

"Then if I should fail, someone else can try again? If I am killed back there, my life too may still be saved?"

He had his answer at once from the gravity of their faces. But they went into explanations: "All that you see being done here, all this work, is just to try to give that one man back his life. If we can restore him, then all the other bent and altered lives surrounding his will also flow back where they were before the berserkers interfered. But not yours, for your life was not there in the original pattern. If you should die in the time of King Ay, that death will be real and final for you. And death will be real and final for all of us here, if you fail in your mission—no one will be able to try again."

One of the perquisites of Derron's new rank was a small private cubicle of an office, and right now he was silently cursing the promotion that had given Lisa such a fine place in which to corner him.

"Whose fault *is* it if not yours?" she was demanding, angry as he had never seen her before. "You admit you're the one who suggested they use Matt. Why didn't you suggest they go back and grab someone else from the past instead?"

So far Derron was keeping his patience. "Operations can't just reach back and pull someone out of history every time they feel like it. Ay's crew are a special case, they're going right back where they belong. And Matt is a special case, he was about to die anyway when he was brought up. Now Operations already *has* brought up a couple of other men who were about to die in their own times, but those two haven't had a chance yet to learn where they are, let alone what the mission they're wanted for is all about. When they are able to understand it, there's a chance they may refuse."

"Refuse? What chance did Matt ever have to refuse to go, when you demanded it of him? He thinks you're some kind of a great hero—he's still like a child in so many ways!"

"Beg your pardon, but he's not a child. Far from it. And he won't be helpless. Before we drop him he'll be trained in everything he'll need, from politics to weapons. And we'll be standing by——"

"Weapons?" Now she was really outraged; she was still like a child herself, in some ways.

"Certainly, weapons. Although we hope he's only going to be in Queensland for a few days and won't get involved in any fighting. We're going to try to have Ay rehabilitated and bring Matt back here before the wedding."

"Wedding!"

Derron hastened on. "Matt can take care of himself, and he can do the job that's expected of him. He's a natural leader. Anyone who can lead Neolithic people——"

"Never mind all that!" Becoming aware that her anger was useless, Lisa was sliding toward the brink of tears. "Of course he can do it! If he must. If he's really the only one who can go. But why were *you* the one to suggest that he be used? Right after I had talked to you about him. Why? Did you just have to make sure that *he* was temporary too?"

"Lisa, no!"

Her eyes were brimming over, and she hurried to the door. "I don't know what you are! I don't know you any more!" And she was gone.

Days ago the plastic membrane, its task completed, had fallen away from his face. The new skin had appeared already weathered, thanks to the Moderns' magic, and with the membrane gone the new beard had grown with fantastic speed for two days before slowing to a normal rate.

Now, on the day he was to be dropped, Matt stood for the

last time in front of the mirror in his room—he was still quartered in the hospital—to get a last good look at his new face. Turning his head from side to side, he pondered Ay's cheeks and nose and chin from different angles.

It was a very different face from the one that had looked back at him out of the still waters of Neolithic ponds; but he wondered if the spirit behind it had also been changed sufficiently. It did not seem to Matt that he was yet possessed of the spirit of a king.

"Just a few more questions, sire," said one of the omnipresent tutors, standing at Matt's elbow. For days now the tutors had conversed with him only in Ay's language, while wearing for him airs of respect suitable for subordinates addressing a warrior chief. Maybe they thought they were helping to change his spirit, but it was only play-acting.

The tutor frowned at his notes. "First, how will you spend the evening of the day of your arrival in Queensland?"

Turning away from the mirror, Matt answered patiently, "That is one of the times we cannot be sure of, where Ay's lifeline is hard to see. I will stay in character as best I can, and try to avoid making decisions, especially big ones. I will use my communicator if I think I need help."

"And if you should happen to meet the dragon-machine that assassinated your predecessor?"

"I will try my best to make it move around, even if this means letting it chase me. So you can find the keyhole to cancel out the dragon with all the harm it has done."

Another tutor who stood near the door said: "Operations will be watching closely, they will do their utmost to pull you out before the dragon can do you harm."

"Yes, yes. And with the sword you are giving me, I will have some chance to defend myself."

The tutors' questioning went on, while the time for the drop neared, and a team of technicians came in to dress Matt. They brought with them the best copies that could be made of the garments Ay had worn when embarking for Queensland.

The costumers treated him more like a statue than a king. When it was time for the finishing touches, one of them complained: "If they've decided at last that we should use the original helmet, where is it?"

77

"Both helmets are out at the Reservoir," the other answered. "The communications people are still working on them."

The tutors kept thinking up more last-minute questions, which Matt kept answering patiently while the dressers put a plastic coverall on him over Ay's clothes, and another officer came to lead him out to the little train that would take him through a tunnel to Reservoir H.

Once before he had ridden on this train, when he had been taken to see the sleeping men and the ship. He had not cared for the train's swaying, and did not expect to enjoy riding the ship. As if in tune with this thought, one of the tutors now looked at his timepiece and handed Matt what Matt knew was an anti-motion-sickness pill.

Halfway to the Reservoir, the train stopped at a place where it had not stopped last time, and two men got on. One was the chief called Time Ops; he and everyone else showed deference to the second man, who Matt recognized from his pictures as the Planetary Commander. The Planetary Commander took the seat facing Matt, and sat there swaying lightly with the car's renewed motion, holding Matt in steady scrutiny.

Matt's face was sweating, but only because of the plastic coverall. So, he was thinking, this is what a king looks like in the flesh. At once heavier and less rock-like than his television image. But this man was after all a Modern king, and so the king-spirit in him was bound to be different from that which had been in Ay.

The ruler of the Moderns asked Matt: "I understand you thought it important to see me before you were dropped?" When there was no immediate response he added: "You understand what I'm saying?"

"Yes, I understand. Learning Ay's language has not driven yours out of my mind. I wanted to see you, to see with my own eyes what it is that makes a man a king." Some of the men in the background wanted to laugh when they heard that; but they were afraid to laugh, and quickly smoothed their faces out into immobility. The Planetary Commander did not laugh or even smile, but only glanced sideways at Time Ops before asking Matt: "They've taught you what to do if the dragon-machine comes after you?"

From the corner of his eye Matt saw Time Ops nod slightly to the Planetary Commander.

"Yes," said Matt. "I am to make the machine chase me, get it to move around as much as possible. You will try to pull me out . . ."

The Planetary Commander nodded with satisfaction as he listened. When the train stopped, he waved the others to get off first, so he and Matt were left alone in the car. Then he said: "I will tell you the real secret of being a king. It is to be ready to lay down your life for your people, whenever and however it is needed." Then he nodded solemnly; he meant what he had said, or he thought he meant it, and maybe he considered it a piece of startling wisdom. His eyes for a moment were lonely and uncertain. Then he put on his public face again, and began to speak in loud words of encouragement, smiling and clapping Matt on the shoulder as they walked off the train together.

Derron was waiting at trackside in the low, rough-hewn cavern, to grip hands with Matt in the style of Ay's time. Matt lo   d for Lisa in the busy little crowd, but except perhaps for Derron, only those were here who had some work to do. In his mi.. Matt associated Lisa and Derron, and sometimes he wondered why these two friends of his did not mate. Maybe he would mate with Lisa himself, if he came back from his mission and she was willing. He had thought on occasion that she would be willing, but there had never been time to find out.

The tutors and other busy men hustled Matt off to wait by himself in a small anteroom. He was told he could get out of the coverall, which he did thankfully. He heard another door open somewhere nearby, and into his room came the smell of the vast body of clean water, the lake being hidden and preserved against the planet's future needs.

On the table in his little waiting room lay the sword which the Modern wizards had designed for him. Matt belted on the scabbard and then drew the weapon, looking at it curiously. The edge appeared to be keen, but no more than naturally so. The unaided eye could see nothing of what the Moderns had once shown him through a microscope—the extra edge, thinning to invisibility even under high magnification, which slid out of the ordinary edge when Matt's hand, and his alone, gripped the hilt. In his hand, this sword pierced ordinary metal like cheese, and armour plate like wood, nor was the blade dulled in doing so. The Moderns said that the secret

79

inner edge had been forged of a single molecule; Matt had no need to understand that, and did not try.

But he had come to understand much, he thought, sheathing the sword again. In recent days, sleeping and waking, Matt had had history, along with other things, poured like a river through his mind. And there was a new strength in his mind which the Moderns had not put there, which they marvelled over and said must be due to his twenty thousand years' passage from the direction of the beginning of the world toward the direction of its end.

With this strength to work on the Moderns' teaching, one of the things he could see very clearly was that in Sirgol's history it was the Moderns who were the odd culture, the misfits. Of course by mere count of years, by languages and institutions, the Moderns were far closer to Ay than Ay was to Matt's original People. But in their basic modes of thinking and feeling, Ay and The People were much the closer, to each other and the rest of humanity.

Only such physical power as the Moderns wielded was ever going to destroy the berserkers—or could ever have created them. But when it came to things of the spirit. the Moderns were stunted children. From their very physical powers came their troubled minds, or from their troubled minds came their power over matter, it was hard to say which. In any case, they had not been able to show Matt how to put on the spirit of a king, which was something he was now required to do.

There was another thing he had come to understand—that the spirits of life were very strong in the universe, or they would long ago have been driven from it by the berserker-machines of accident and disease, if not by the malignant ones which came in metal bodies.

Wishing to reach toward the source of life for the help he needed, Matt now did what Ay would have done before embarking on a dangerous voyage—he raised his hands in the wedge-sign of Ay's religion and murmured a brief prayer, expressing his needs and feelings in the form Ay would have used.

That done, he could see no reason to stay shut up any longer in this little room. So he opened the door and stepped out.

Everyone was as busy as before. Men worked, singly or in groups, on various kinds of gear. Others hurried past, this way and that, calling out orders or information. Most of them remained utterly intent on their business, but a few faces were turned toward Matt; the faces were annoyed that he had come popping out of his container before it was time for him to be used, fearful lest he cause some disruption of the schedule.

After one look around, he ignored the faces. Ay's helmet was waiting for him on a stand, and he went to it and picked it up. With his own hands he set the silver-winged thing upon his head.

It was an unplanned, instinctive gesture; the faces watching were enough to show him that the instinct had been right. The men looking on fell into an unwilling silence that was mirror enough to show Matt that the helmet had marked a transformation, even though in another moment the men were turning back to their jobs with busy practicality, ignoring as best they could the new presence in their midst.

In another moment, some of his tutors came hurrying up again, saying that they had just a few more questions. Matt understood they felt a sudden need to reassure themselves that they were his teachers still, and not his subjects. But now that the spirit he needed had come to him, he was not going to give them any such comfort; the tutors' time of power over him had passed.

Looking for the Planetary Commander, he strode impatiently through the knots of busy people. Some of them looked up, angry at his jostling, but when they beheld him they fell silent and made way. He walked into the group where the ruler of the Moderns was standing, and stood looking down into his wrinkle-circled eyes.

"I grow impatient," said Matt. "Are my ship and my men ready, or are they not?"

And the Planetary Commander looked back with a surprise that became something like envy before he nodded.

On his earlier trip to the Reservoir Matt had seen Ay's crew lying asleep in specially constructed beds, while machines stretched their muscles to keep them strong, lamps threw slivers of sunlight on their faces and arms to keep them tanned, and electronic familiars whispered tirelessly to them that their young lord lived.

This time the men were on their feet, though they moved like sleepwalkers, eyes still shut. They had been dressed again

81

in their own clothes, and armed again with their own harness and weapons. Now they were being led in a long file from Lukas's manor down to the beach and hoisted aboard their ship. The gunwale that had been scraped by dragon-scales had been replaced, and everything else maintained.

The fog-generators had long ago been turned off. Every man and object on the thin crescent of beach stood centred in a flower of shadow-petals, in the light of the cold little suns that clustered high up under the black distant curve of roof.

Matt shook Derron's hand again, and other offered hands, then waded briefly through the fresh water and swung himself up on the long-ship's deck. A machine was coming to push the craft out into deep water.

Time Ops came climbing on board with Matt, and half-followed, half-led him on a quick tour of inspection that finally took both of them into the royal tent.

"...stick to your briefing, especially regarding the dragon. Try to make it move around as much as possible—if you should see it. Remember that historical damage, even casualties, are of secondary importance if we can find the dragon's keyhole. Then everything can be set right..."

Time Ops' voice trailed off as Matt turned to face him, holding in his hands a replica of the winged helmet on his head, a replica he had just picked up from atop Ay's treasure chest. "I have heard all your lectures before," said Matt. "Now take this, and compose a lecture on carelessness for those whom you command."

Time Ops grabbed the helmet, glaring at it in anger that for the moment was speechless.

"And now," said Matt, "get off my ship unless you mean to pull an oar."

Still gripping the helmet and muttering to himself, Time Ops was already on his way.

After that, Matt paid the Modern world no more attention. He went to stand beside Harl, who had been set like a sleepy statue beside the steering oar. The other men, still tranced, were in place on their benches. Their hands moved slightly on their oars' worn wood as if glad to be back, making sure they were where they really fitted.

Looking out past the prow, over the black water under the distant lights, Matt heard a hum of power behind him and felt the ship slide free. In the next moment he saw a shimmering circle grow beneath her—and then, with scarcely a splash, the darkness and the cave were gone, exploded into a glare of blue light. An open morning sky gave seabirds room to wheel away, crying their surprise at the sudden appearance of a ship. Free salt air blew in Matt's face, and a groundswell passed under his feet. Dead ahead, the horizon was marked with the blue vague line he had been told to expect—Queensland. Off to starboard, a reddened sun was just climbing clear of dawn.

Matt spent no time with last thoughts or hesitations. "Harl!" he roared out, at the same time thwacking his steersman so hard on the shoulder that he nearly toppled even as his eyes broke open. "Must I watch alone all day, as well as through the end of the night?"

He had been told that these words in his voice would wake the men, and so it happened. The warriors blinked and growled their way out of their long slumber, each man perhaps thinking that he alone had dozed briefly at his oar. Most of them had started rowing before their spirits were fully back in control of their bodies, but within a few seconds they had put a ragged stroke together, and in a few seconds more all of them were pulling strongly and smoothly.

Matt moved between the benches, making sure all were fully awake, bestowing curses and half-affectionate slaps such as no one else but Ay would dare give these men. Before they had been given time to start thinking, to wonder what they had been doing five minutes ago, they were firmly established in a familiar routine. And if, against commended forgetfulness, any man's mind still harboured visions of an attacking dragon and a slaughtered chief, no doubt that man would be more than glad to let such nightmare vapours vanish with the daylight.

"Row, boys! Ahead is the land where, they say, all women are queens!"

It was a good harbour they found waiting for them. This was Blanium, Queensland's capital, a town of some eight or ten thousand folk, a big city in this age. Immediately inland from the harbour, on the highest point of hill, there rose the grey keep of a small castle. From those high battlements the Princess Alix was doubtless now peering down at the ship, to catch a first distant look at her husband-to-be.

In the harbour there were other vessels, traders and wanderers, but only eight or ten of them; few for the season and for all the length of quay. Empire trade was falling off steadily over the years, seamen and landsmen alike faced evil days. But let Ay live, and a part of the civilized world would outlast the storm.

In scattered rivulets folk were dribbling down Blanium's steep streets, to form a throng along the quay as the long-ship entered the harbour. By the time his crew had pulled into easy hailing distance, and the cheers on shore had started, Matt beheld nearly a thousand people of all ranks waiting to see him land. From the castle, whence of course the ship must have been spied a great distance out, there had come down two large chariots of gilded wood, drawn by hump-backed load-beasts. These had halted near the water's edge, where men of some high rank had dismounted and now stood waiting.

The moment of arrival came, of songs and tossed flowers of welcome. Ropes were thrown ashore, and a crew of dockmen made the long-ship fast to bollards on the quay, riding against a bumper of straw mats. Matt leaped ashore, concealing his relief at escaping the rise and fall of the sea. It was probably a good thing for Ay's reputation that the voyage had been no longer.

The delegation of nobles earnestly bade him welcome, a sentiment echoed by the crowd. King Gorboduc sent his regret that he ailed too much to come down to the harbour himself, and his wish to see Ay as soon as possible in the castle. Matt knew that Gorboduc was old, and ill indeed, having only about a month to live, historically, beyond this day.

The king was still without a male heir, and the Queensland nobles would not long submit to the rule of any woman. And for Alix to marry one of them might displease the others enough to bring on the very civil war that she and her father were seeking so desperately to avoid. So, logically enough, the king's thoughts had turned to Ay—a princely man of royal blood, young and extremely capable, respected if not liked by all, with no lands of his own to divide his loyalty.

Leaving orders for Harl to see to the unloading of the ship and the quartering of the crew, Matt took from Ay's coffer the jewels historically chosen by Ay as gifts for king and princess. And then he accepted a chariot ride up the hill.

In the Moderns' world he had heard of places in the universe where loadbeasts came in shapes that allowed men to straddle and ride them. He was just as well satisfied that such was not the case on Sirgol. Learning to drive a chariot had presented problems enough, and today he was happy to leave the reins in another's hands. Matt hung on with one hand and used the other to wave to the crowds; as the chariots clattered up through the steep streets of the town, more hundreds of citizens, of all classes, came pouring out of the buildings and byways to salute Matt with cries of welcome. The people expected the sea-rover to hold their country together; he hoped they were making no mistake.

The high grey walls of the castle at last loomed close. The chariots rumbled over a drawbridge, and pulled to a halt in a narrow courtyard inside the castle walls. Here Matt was saluted by the sword and pike of the guard, and acknowledged the greetings of a hundred minor officials and gentry.

In the great hall of the castle there were gathered only a score of men and women, but these naturally were the most important. When Matt was ushered in to the sound of trumpet and drum, only a few of these showed anything like the enthusiasm of the crowds outside. Matt could recognize most of the faces here, from their likenesses in old portraits and secret photos; and he knew from the Modern historians that for the most part these powerful people were suspending judgement on Ay—and that there were a few among them whose smiles were totally false. The leader of this last faction would be the court wizard Nomis, who stood tall in a white robe such as Colonel Lukas had worn, wearing a smile that seemed no more than a baring of teeth.

If there was pure joy anywhere, it shone in the lined and wasted face of King Gorboduc. To cry welcome he rose from his chair of state, though his legs would support him only for a moment. After embracing Matt and exchanging formal greetings the wheezing king sank back into his seat. His narrow-eyed scrutiny continued, giving Matt the feeling that his disguise was being probed.

"Young man," Gorboduc quavered suddenly. "You look very like your father. He and I shared many a fight and many a feast; may he rouse well in the Warriors' Castle, tonight and always."

Ay would receive such a wish with mixed feelings, and Ay was ever the man to speak out what he felt. "I thank you, Gorboduc, for meaning to wish my father well. May his spirit rest forever in the Garden of the Blessed above."

Gorboduc was taken with a sudden coughing spell; perhaps he gave way to it more fully than need be, to spare himself making an issue of this correction from an upstart in his own hall.

But Nomis was not about to let his chance slip by. He strode forward, white robe flowing, while the king was momentarily incapacitated in the hands of his attendants.

Nomis did not speak to Matt directly, but stood beside him in the front of the hall and addressed the others. "You lords of the realm! Will all of you stand silent while the gods of your fathers are thus insulted?"

Most of them would, it seemed. Perhaps they were not sure of the insult; perhaps not of the gods. A few of them did grumble something, but low enough to be ignored.

Matt, his nerves stretched taut, did not ignore them. "I meant no insult to any here," he said clearly. The conciliatory words were hardly out of his mouth before he felt sure that they had been a mistake, too mild an utterance, too near an apology to have come from the real Ay. Nomis displayed a faint sneer of pleasure, and some of the others were suddenly looking at Matt with new expressions of calculation; the atmosphere had subtly changed.

The king had recovered from his coughing fit, and now all other matters must wait while his daughter was led forth by her attendant women. From behind a gauzy veil, Alix's eyes smiled briefly at Matt before being modestly lowered; and he thought that the Moderns had spoken truly, there would be many worse lifelines than Ay's to follow to the end.

While preparations were being made for the exchange of gifts, a friendly noble whispered to Matt that if the Lord Ay had no objection, the king preferred that the betrothal ceremony be completed at once. It would mean unusual haste, but there was the matter of the king's health . . .

"I understand." Matt looked toward the princess. "If Alix is agreeable, I am."

Her eyes, intense and warm, flicked at him again. And in a

few more minutes he and she were standing side by side with joined hands.

With a show of great reluctance being overcome only by a loyalty that was stronger still, Nomis came at the king's order to perform the ceremony of formal betrothal. Midway through, he raised his eyes to the audience when asking the ritual question, whether anyone present had objection to the proposed marriage. And the wizard showed not the least surprise when a loud answer came from one at whom he was staring.

"I—I do object! I have long sought the princess for my own. And I think the sea-rover will be better mated with my sword!"

The deep voice had hesitated and stammered at the start, and it was perhaps a shade too loud for real confidence to be behind it. But the speaker looked formidable enough, young and tall and wide-shouldered, with arms thick enough to make the average man a pair of legs.

Gorboduc no doubt would have liked to intervene, and forbid a duel, but he could not in the case of a formal betrothal challenge. There was no historical record of Ay's having fought a duel at his betrothal ceremony, an item not likely to have been overlooked by the chroniclers; but still Nomis had now pushed his pawn forward. For this Matt supposed he could blame only himself, for somehow failing to match Ay's exact behaviour, and so encouraging the challenge.

Anyway, there was no doubt about what had to be done now. Matt hooked his thumbs into his wide leather belt, faced his challenger, and drew a deep breath. "Will you state your name?"

The young giant answered in a tense voice, his tone far more hesitant than his words. "I need no introduction to any person of quality here. But that you may address me with the proper respect, know that I am Yunguf, of the House of Yung. And know also that I claim the Princess Alix for my own."

Matt bowed. He was very smooth and cool, as Ay would be. "Since you appear to be a worthy man, Yunguf, we may fight at once to decide this matter. If you have no reason to delay?"

Yunguf flushed; his control slipped for a moment and Matt saw that beneath it the man was certainly badly frightened— more frightened than such a warrior should be by any duel.

The princess's hand fell on Matt's arm; she had put her veil aside, and now, looking soberly at Matt, she drew him a little aside and spoke to him in a low voice. "I hope with all my heart that you fare well in this matter, lord. My affections have never belonged to that man."

"Princess, has he ever asked to marry you?"

"A year ago he did." Alix's eye flickered in maidenly modesty. "As others have. But when I said him nay he never pressed the matter more."

"So." Matt looked across the hall to where Nomis was now intoning a blessing of the Old Religion over Yunguf's arms. Yunguf seemed to need all his courage, to keep from shrinking away from the wizard's touch. No, it was not simple death or wounding in a duel that Yunguf feared.

Matt himself could face the personal danger calmly enough. He had spent most of his life within reach of violence from animals or nature, though as one of The People he had very rarely been in danger from another human being. The Moderns had given him Ay's lithe hitting power and endurance, had put not only skill but extra speed into his nerves. And they had given him his special sword, which alone could be advantage enough to win a fight. No, it was not Yunguf's prowess that bothered Matt, it was the very fact of the duel, and the changes in history that it must bring.

Save for the king and princess and the two participants, everyone seemed happy at the prospect of a little bloodletting. There was general impatience at the delay necessary for Ay's shield to be fetched up from the ship. This delay would have allowed Matt time to get away by himself for a minute and report to Operations; but there was nothing he could say to them, or they to him, that would get him out of the duel. So, Matt passed the time in trying to make light conversation with the ladies, while Yunguf stood glowering and almost silent with a group who seemed to be his relatives.

The shield was soon brought in by Harl, who entered running, displaying every sign of eagerness to see the fight get started—probably with the idea of unsettling his lord's opponent's nerves as much as possible.

The company moved outside, where they were joined enthusiastically by the minor nobility and such of the commons as could crowd within sight. The king, chair and all, was established in the best vantage point, with the higher nobles round him. This courtyard was evidently consecrated to weaponry, judging by the massive timber butts, much hacked and splintered, which stood along its farther side.

The noble who had whispered to Matt about the betrothal came whispering again, to ask if he was acceptable to the Lord Ay as referee; Matt nodded his agreement.

"Then, my lord, if you will take a stand in the arena."

Matt moved to the centre of the clear paved space, which was large enough to allow a good deal of manoeuvring, and drew his blade. When he saw Yunguf advancing on him with blade and shield ready, slow and powerful-looking as a siege tower, he understood that there would be no further preliminaries. It seemed that at Gorboduc's court killing was much less ritualized than wedding.

The sun had passed the zenith by now, the air was warm, and in the windless courtyard even moderate exercise soon raised a sweat. Yunguf's approach, with many feints, was slow and cautious almost to the point of parody, but no one watching showed surprise. Probably a feigned slowness at the start was Yunguf's usual style. Sure enough, he moved quickly at last, and Matt stepped quickly back, his shield, sword, shield, parrying in good order the three blows of the attacking combination. Matt had hoped that at the clash of blades his opponent's sword might break, but the contact had been flatsided and glancing and Yunguf's weapon was evidently tough. And, Matt realized now, if one sword was broken another would be provided; if two or three, cries of sorcery would be raised. No, only wounds could now decide the issue.

Matt worked his way back to the middle of the arena, still keeping out of Yunguf's way. The knowledge weighed on him that any killing he did today, any wounds he carved, would be disruptive change that worked to the advantage of the berserkers. But for Matt to be killed or beaten by Yunguf would damage history still more. The onlookers had already begun to murmur; no doubt his deep reluctance for this brawl was showing. He had to win, and the sooner the better—but without killing or maiming, if that were possible.

Matt raised his sword and shield in readiness as Yunguf moved slowly into attacking range, and when Yunguf charged again, Matt beat him to the thrust, aiming along the side of Yunguf's shield to damage the sword-arm's shoulder-muscles.

But Yunguf was twisting his body with the force of his own lunge; as the huge man's blade slid off Matt's shield, Yunguf's body turned into the way of Matt's thrust, which cut between his upper ribs.

The wound was only moderately deep, and Yunguf was not yet stopped, but his next slash was weak and slow. Matt swayed back just enough to let the blow go by, then lunged in again, blocking sword with sword, hooking the wounded man's knee with his foot, using his shield to force Yunguf's upper body back.

Yunguf fell like a tree, and there was Matt's bloody point hovering at his throat, while Matt's foot pinned Yunguf's sword-wrist to the paving stone.

"Will you—yield to me—the combat—and its prize?" Matt was now aware of his own panting, and of Yunguf's whistling, strangely gurgling breath.

"I yield me." The answer, in strangled tones, came quickly enough. There were no grounds for hesitation.

Matt stepped wearily back, wondering what Ay customarily used to wipe a bloody swordblade. Harl came to perform that office for him, and to scold him about his hesitancy at the start of the fight. Yunguf's relatives had gone to Yunguf's aid, and with their help the wounded man seemed to be sitting up easily enough. At least, thought Matt, a killing had been avoided.

He turned to the princess and her father, to find them with frightened eyes fixed on an object that had been discarded on the ground nearby. It was Nomis's outer robe, snowy in the sunlight. The wizard himself was no longer in sight; the white garment discarded was a plain enough signal that he was donning black.

A cough sounded wetly behind Matt, and he turned to see Yunguf with bright blood upon his lips.

The great metal dragon lay motionless, buried almost completely in the muck of the sea bottom. Around it the dull life of the great depths stirred—in safety, for this berserker was now seeking to avoid killing anything. For it to end even a vegetable lifeline non-historically could provide a datum for the Moderns' huge computers, implacable as berserkers themselves, to use in their relentless search for the dragon's keyhole.

The dragon was still under the direct command of the berserker fleet which was besieging the planet in Modern times. On their own version of sentry screens that fleet's linked computers had observed the lifting of Ay's ship and crew to Modern times, and their subsequent restoration to Ay's time, with one lifeline added.

It was obvious what the Moderns intended, obvious to machines who themselves knew well the theory and practice of baiting traps. But a viable replacement for Ay was bait they could not afford to ignore. They must strike again, using one of the dragon's weapons.

But this time they must be subtle. Matt must not be killed, at least not in any way that would spin a new thread of causation toward the dragon for the Moderns to follow. The linked berserker computers pondered electrically, and arrived at what they considered an ideal solution: Capture Matt alive, and hold him so, until the pillars of Sirgol's history came crashing down.

Even while in hiding, the dragon maintained around itself a net of subtle infraelectronic senses. Among the things it now observed in this way was a black-robed man, standing on a pillar of seaside rock about two miles from the berserker's hiding place, speaking on and on rhythmically, into the empty air. From data in its memory banks the berserker deduced that this man was attempting to call supernatural forces to his aid.

And in the man's speech it caught the name of Ay.

In the full sunlight of mid-afternoon Nomis stood chanting on his pinnacle of rock. The spells of deepest evil were best sung in darkness, but his hate and fear had grown until they seemed to spread a darkness of their own about him. He would not wait for the setting of the sun.

While the seabirds wheeled round him, crying in the wind, he sang in his thin penetrating voice:

> "Demon of darkness, rise and stalk
> Put on the bones and make them walk
> Dead men's bones through the weed and slime
> Walk and climb
> Walk to me here
> Speak to me here
> Of the secret to bring my enemy's death."

There was more, much more, all cajoling and coercing the dark wet things that waited in the deeps for men to drown—waited for fresh-drowned bones to come falling through the fathoms, for limber young corpses that the demons could wear like clothes in their endless revels at the bottom of the sea. The dark wet things down there possessed all the knowledge of death, including how the death of Ay might be accomplished—something Yunguf had proven unable to achieve, despite all the supernatural threats Nomis had lavished on the lout.

Nomis's thin arms quivered, holding drowned men's fingers over his head. Then his arms swept low as he bowed, still chanting, eyelids closing out the sun. Today the spells would work, today the hatred was in him like a lodestone, drawing to him things of utter evil.

When he came to a place in the chant where he could pause, he did so. He let down his arms and opened his eyes, wondering if he had heard another sound between the surges of the surf. Under his black robe his old man's chest was heaving with exertion and excitement.

A bird screamed. And from below, from somewhere on the furrowed length of cliff that climbed to this tabletop from the sea, there came once more a scraping sound, almost lost in wind and surf.

He had just given up listening for a repetition, and started to chant again, when from much nearer the top of the cliff, from almost under Nomis's feet, there came a small clatter, a tumble of stones dislodged by some climbing foot or hand. The sound was in itself so ordinary that it momentarily drove all thoughts of magic from the magician's tired mind. He could only think angrily that someone was about to discover his hideaway.

Before him as he faced the sea was a cleft that climbed to the tabletop between folds of rock. From just out of sight within this cleft there now came the sound of grit crunched under a heavy foot.

And then Nomis's world was shaken around him, by a proof that put an end to a lifetime's nagging inward doubts. His first glimpse of his climbing visitor showed him a drowned man's skull, one small tendril of seaweed clinging to its glistening crown.

With quick smooth movements the whole form climbed into

his view. It was a man-form, thinner than any living human but fuller than any skeleton. Drowned skeletons must change when a demon possessed them—this one looked more like metal than bone.

Having emerged completely from the crevice, the demon-shape halted. It stood taller than tall Nomis, so that it bent its skull-head down slightly on its cable neck to look at him. He had to struggle not to turn and run, to stand his ground and make himself keep looking into the cloudy jewels that were its eyes. A drop of water sparkled, falling from one bone-like fingertip. Only when the thing took another step toward him did Nomis remember to reinforce his chalked protective ring with a gesture and a muttered incantation.

And then at last he also remembered to complete his astoundingly successful ritual with a binding spell. "Now you must guide and serve me, until you are released! And serve me first by saying how my enemy can be put to death."

The shiny jaw did not move, but a quavery voice came forth from a black square where the mouth should have been. "Your enemy is Ay. He landed today upon this coast."

"Yes, yes. And the secret of his death?"

Even for the berserker to order another to accomplish Matt's death would leave a track of causation on the Moderns' screens. "You must bring your enemy Ay here, alive and unhurt, and give him to me. Then you will never see him more. And if you do this I will help you gain whatever else you may desire."

Nomis's mind raced. He had trained himself for nearly a lifetime, to seize such an opportunity as this, and he was not going to fail now, not going to be tricked or cheated. So, the demon wanted Ay kept alive! That could only mean that some vital magical connection existed between the sea-rover and this thing from the deeps. That Ay should have enjoyed such help in his career was far from surprising, considering the number of men he had sent to dwell among the fishes, and the charmed life he himself seemed to bear.

Nomis's voice came out harsh and bold. "What is Ay to you, demon?"

"My enemy."

Not likely! Nomis almost laughed the words aloud. He realized now that it was his own body and soul that the wet thing craved; but behind his spells and his chalked circle he was protected. The demon had come to protect Ay. But Nomis would not let the demon know how much he had deduced. Not yet. He saw in this situation possibilities of gain so enormous as to be worth any risk.

"Harken, mud-thing! I will do as you ask. Tonight at midnight I will bring your enemy here, bound and helpless. Now begone, and return at midnight, ready to grant me all I ask!"

In the evening Matt went walking with Alix along the battlements, watching the stars come out, while the princess's ladies-in-waiting hovered just out of sight around corners.

Matt's preoccupation with his inner thoughts was evidently obvious. The girl beside him soon gave up a rather one-sided effort to make small talk, and asked him plainly: "Do I please you, lord?"

He stopped his moody pacing and turned to her. "Princess, you please me very well indeed." And it was so. "If my thoughts go elsewhere, it is only because they are forced."

She smiled sympathetically. The Moderns would not think Alix a beautiful girl. But Matt all his life had seen women's beauty under sunburn and woodsmoke and toughness, and he could see beauty now in this different girl of his third world.

"May I know then, lord, what problem forces your thoughts away?"

"For one thing, the problem of the man I wounded. I have not made a good beginning here."

"Such concern does you credit. I am pleased to discover you more gentle than I had been led to expect." Alix smiled again. No doubt she understood that his concern over Yunguf rested mainly on reasons of policy; though she could of course have no idea of how very far that policy ranged. She began to tell Matt of some things that she might do, people she could talk to, to help heal the breach between the new house of Ay and that of Yung.

Listening, and watching her, he felt he could be king in truth if she were queen beside him. He would not be Ay. He knew now, as the Moderns surely must, that no man could really live another's life. But in Ay's name, he might perhaps be king enough to serve the world.

He interrupted Alix. "And do you find me pleasing, lady?"

This time her marvellous eyes did more than flicker; with a warm light of promise they held fast to his. And as if by instinct the duennas came at that moment to announce that the decent time-limit for keeping company had been reached.

"Until the morning, then," he said, taking the princess's hand briefly, in the way permitted by courtly manners.

"Until the morning, my lord." And as the women led her away, she turned back to send him another glance of promise before passing out of sight.

He stood there alone, gazing after the princess, wishing to see her for ten thousand mornings more, then he took off his helmet for a moment, and rubbed his head. His communicator was still silent. No doubt he should call in to Operations and report all that had happened.

Instead he put the helmet on again (Ay would wear it as a sort of dress uniform) and went down into the keep, to find his way to the chamber where Yunguf had been bedded down on orders of the court physician. Through the doorway of the room he saw a pair of the wounded man's relatives on watch inside, and he hesitated to enter. But when they saw Matt they beckoned him in, speaking to him freely and courteously. None of the House of Yung, it seemed, were likely to bear him any ill-will for winning a duel.

Yunguf was pale and looked somehow shrunken. His difficult breath gurgled in his throat, and when he twisted on his pallet to spit up blood, the bandage loosened from his wound and air gurgled there also with his breath. He showed no fear now, but when Matt asked him how he did, Yunguf whispered that he was dying. There was more he wanted to say to Matt, but talking came too hard.

"Lord Ay," said one of the relatives reluctantly, "I think my cousin would say that his challenge to you was a lie, and that therefore he knew he could not win."

The man on the pallet nodded.

"Also——" The cousin paused, when the other relative gestured at him worriedly. Then he went on, in a determined rush of words. "I think Yunguf would warn you that things harder to fight against than swords are set against you here."

"I saw the white robe, left on the ground."

"Ah, then you are warned. May your new god defend you if a time comes when your sword will avail nothing."

A sea-bird cried in the night outside. Yunguf's eyes, fear in them again, turned to the small window.

Matt wished the men of Yung well and climbed the stair back to the castle roof. He could be alone there, and unobserved, since only a token watch was kept, and full night had now descended. Once secluded in lonely darkness, he took a deep breath, and for the first time pressed his helmet's right wing in a certain way, switching on the communicator.

"Time Ops here." The crisp Modern voice was barely a whisper of sound, but it made the castle, and even the open night with its rising moon, somehow unreal. Reality was once more a grimly crowded cave-fortress, at the centre of a fantastic web of machines and energy. In what sounded to his own ears like a lifeless voice, Matt reported the duel and Nomis's departure, with the implied threat of the discarded white robe.

"Yes, our screens showed Yunguf's lifeline being hit by something. He's going to——" A paradox-loop censored out some words of Time Ops' speech. "Nothing vital is involved there, though." By that Time Ops of course meant that nothing vital to the Moderns' historical base was involved. "Have you seen or heard anything of the dragon yet?"

"No." The track of the rising moon showed the sea calm out to the distant horizon. "Why do you speak of the dragon so much?"

"Why?" The tiny voice seemed to crackle. "Because it's important!"

"Yes, I know. But what about my task here, of being king? If you help me I can do that, though it seems that I cannot be Ay."

There was a pause. "You're doing as well as can be expected, Matt. We'll tell you when there's corrective action you must take, to stay closer to Ay's lifeline. Yes, you're doing a damn good job, from what our screens show. As I said, what happens to Yunguf isn't vital. Your watching out for that dragon is."

"I will watch out for it, of course."

After routinely breaking off the contact, Matt decided it was time he visited Ay's men, who had been quartered temporarily in a kind of guardroom built into the castle's massive outer wall. With this in mind he descended from the keep along an outer stair.

He was deep in thought, and it did not occur to him that the courtyard at the bottom of the stair was darker than it ought to have been. Nor did he wonder that the postern gate nearby stood half-open and unguarded. A sound of rapid movement at his rear alerted him, but too late; before he could draw sword a wave of men were on him, weighing him down. And before he could shed Ay's pride enough to utter a cry for help, something smothering had been bound tight around his head.

"Sir, can you spare a minute? It's important."

Time Ops looked up impatiently from behind his desk, but paused when he saw Derron's face, and what he was carrying. "Come in, then, major. What is it?"

Derron walked stiffly into the office, carrying a winged helmet under his arm. "Sir, I've been—sort of hanging onto this. It's the extra one Matt found on his ship before he was dropped. Today some communications people came to see me about it. There was a continuous noise-signal being generated in its chrono-transmitter."

Time Ops just sat there behind his desk, waiting not too patiently for Derron to get to the point.

"The communications people told me, sir, that the signal from this helmet was interfering with a similar signal put out by the helmet Matt's wearing. Whichever one he'd taken, he'd be walking around back there broadcasting a built-in noise, very easy for the berserker to identify as a chrono-transmitter and home in on. The berserker must have thought it an obvious trap, sir, since it hasn't homed in and killed him yet." Derron's voice was very well controlled, but he could feel his anger in the tightness of his throat.

"So, you're shocked at what we're doing, Odegard. Is that it?" Time Ops grew angry too, but not guiltily or defensively. He was only angry, it seemed, with Derron's obtuseness. He flicked on his desk screen and spun a selector. "Take a look at this. Our present view of Ay's lifeline."

During his hitch of sentry duty Derron had got pretty good at reading the screens. This was the first look he had had today at what was happening to Ay's lifeline. He studied the picture carefully, but what he saw only confirmed his fears of yesterday. "It looks bad. He's getting way off the track."

"Matt's buying a little more present-time for us here, and so far that's all he's doing. Is it clear now why we're trying to get dragon to kill him? Millions, many millions, have died in war for *nothing*, major."

"I see." His anger was growing more choking by the moment, because there was nowhere it could justly be vented. In hands that he could not keep from shaking, Derron held the helmet out in front of him for a moment, looking at it as if it was an archeological find he had just unearthed. "I see. You'll never win unless you find that dragon's keyhole. Matt never was anything but a fancy piece of live bait, was he?"

"No, I wouldn't say that, major." Time Ops' voice was less sharp. "When you first suggested that he be used, we weren't sure but that he could come out alive. But the first full-scale computer-simulation showed us the way things pretty well had to go. No doubt you're right when you say bugging the helmet made the trap a little too obvious." Time Ops shrugged, a slight, tired motion. "The way things stand at this moment, Matt may just be safer from berserkers than we are."

Matt came painfully awake, trying to cough around a gag of dirty cloth that had been stuffed into his mouth. His head ached, throbbing hideously, as if he had been drugged. He was being carried in a sickening jogging motion, and when his head had cleared a little more he understood that he was riding slung across a loadbeast's humped back, his head hanging down on one side of the animal and his feet on the other. His helmet of course had fallen off somewhere, nor was there any bouncing tug at his waist from the weight of sword and scabbard.

Six or eight men had him prisoner. They were walking near the loadbeast in the darkness, guiding and leading it along a narrow winding path by moonlight. The men looked behind them frequently, and now and then exchanged a few low-voiced words.

"I think two of them are following, or they were . . ."

Matt heard that much. He tried the cords holding his wrists and ankles, and found them strong and tight. Turning his head, he could see that the trail ahead wound among jagged pillars and outcroppings of rock; from what he knew of the country near Blanium he judged that they were right along the coast.

When the man who was leading the way turned and paused

a moment to let the others close up, Matt saw without surprise that he was tall and thin and robed in black, and had belted round his lean waist a sword and scabbard that looked like Matt's. Nomis had taken for himself one of the power-symbols of a king.

The way grew steadily rougher. Shortly the little procession came to a thin ridge, with deep clefts in the rock on either side of it; here the loadbeast must be left behind. At Nomis's order some of the men lifted Matt from its back. He tried to feign unconsciousness, but Nomis came to lift his eyelids and then regard him with a knowing grin.

"He's awake. Untie his feet, but see to it that his arms are doubly secure."

The men did so. The further they progressed on this hike the more often they stopped to look uneasily about them, starting at every sound of the night. They seemed to fear Nomis and whatever lay ahead almost as much as they feared the pursuit that must be coming after them from the castle.

With his arms still bound behind his back, men ahead and behind holding on to him, Matt was led across the single-file ridge, then made to scramble up through a long twisting chute, almost a tunnel between high walls of rock that shaded out the moon. Only Nomis, leading through the darkness, seemed to know the way. The sound of surf became audible, drifting from somewhere below.

A cloud was over the moon when the party straggled at last onto a tiny tableland of rock. Only Nomis immediately saw the figure which had been waiting, motionless as stone, for their arrival. When he saw it, he quickly drew Matt's sword; and when Matt was pushed up out of the chute within his reach he gripped Matt's hair with one hand and with the other laid the bare blade against Matt's throat.

The moon came out then, and the other men saw the thing that stood watching them. Like odd chicks of some gaunt black bird, they squawked and scrambled then to get behind Nomis, all making sure they were within the old chalked diagram. For a few seconds, then, everything was still, save for the faint wind and the surf, and one man's muttering in fear.

Keeping the sword against Matt's neck, Nomis pulled the gag from his face and displayed him to the berserker. "What say you, mud-thing, is this man indeed your enemy? Shall I slay him, then?"

The metal puppet might have been sent charging forward, far faster than any man could move, to pull Matt away to captivity. But there was the keen edge right against the jugular. The berserkers would not risk a thread of responsibility for Matt's death.

"Wizard, I will give you power," said the demon. "And wealth, and the pleasures of the flesh, and then life everlasting. But first you must give me that man alive."

Nomis crooned in his certainty of victory, while at his back his men huddled in terror. In this moment when all desires seemed possible of attainment, there rose uppermost in his mind the memory of a day long ago, when a child-princess's mocking laughter had burned at him. "I want Alix," he whispered. To him the breaking of her pride would mean more than her young body.

"I will give her to you," lied the demon solemnly, "when you have given me that man alive."

In Nomis's ecstasy of triumph his arm wavered slightly, holding the long sword. Matt was ready. His bound wrists allowed him still some arm-movement, and as he jerked free with all his strength his elbow struck old ribs with force enough to send Nomis sprawling, and the sword spinning in the air.

The other men's terror was triggered into panic flight. They burst up from their crouched positions, first scattering blindly and then converging on the only path of escape, the narrow way by which they had ascended. Running straight, head down, Matt kicked the fallen sword ahead of him and still got there first by a stride, thanks to what the Moderns had done for his nerves and muscles.

The berserker was delayed by its need to avoid mangling the men who got in its way, but even as Matt reached the top of the path he felt a hand harder than flesh scrape down his back. It seized his clothing but the fabric tore free. Then he was leaping, falling into the descending passage. At his back the other men were screaming in raw fear as they collided with one another and with the berserker.

When he landed he naturally fell, cutting and bruising himself without really feeling the injuries. The way was so narrow that he could not miss finding the sword he had kicked ahead of him. With his bound hands he groped behind him in the dark to pick it up by the blade, heedless of nicked fingers. Then he got his feet under him and scrambled some further distance downward. He stumbled and fell again, hurting his knee, but he had gained a substantial lead on the tangled terror that was jamming the narrow chute behind him. One or more men had probably fallen with broken bones or other disabling injuries, and the others were stuck with them or behind them. They were all howling with mindless fear, and no doubt lacerating themselves further in the dark when they felt the chill touch of the berserker; it would be sorting through men to find the one it wanted, trying to get the others out of its way without doing them damage.

Matt propped the swordblade behind him, and with the skill of his new nerves slid his bonds against its edge. He had freed himself before he heard the machine's footsteps come crunching down towards him in the dark.

"That's it, that's it, we'll nail the damned thing now!" In Time Operations men were crying out a hunters' jubilation that was as old as mankind. On their screens their giant computers were limning out the radii of a spiderweb, whose centre would hold the dragon. The data needed to draw the web was flowing in from human lifelines being bent and battered; the berserker seemed to be struggling with men in some enclosed space.

But still it had not killed again. And the locus of its keyhole was not yet in sight.

"Only a little more." Time Ops, staring wildly at his screens, pleaded for bloodshed. "Something?"

But there was no more.

Matt retreated, limping, getting out into the moonlight where he could see. The thing followed unhurriedly, sure of him now. He backed out onto the thin ridge, between yawning crevices too deep for the moonlight to plumb, gripping his sword's hilt in bleeding fingers. Pale in the moonlight and almost skeleton-thin, the machine followed him carefully. It did not want him to fall. It would choose the precise moment and then rush to catch him, easily as a human athlete picking up a toddler from a broad walk.

He kept his point centred on the narrow way that it would have to come, and he had just time enough to steel his arm. A moment ago the berserker had been twelve feet away, and now it was on him. It made a wiping motion with one hand, to clear what appeared to be an ordinary swordblade from its path—and four steel fingers leaped free like small silver fish in the moonlight, while the monomolecular blade stayed where it was, centred by Matt's braced muscles.

The inertia of the machine's rush was great. Before it could halt itself, the swordpoint had gone through its torso, and what had been delicately controlled mechanism became dead hurtling weight. Matt went down before the force of it, but he clung to rock somehow, and saw it go on over him, falling in an endless slow somersault, taking with it the transfixing sword, which glowed already like a redhot needle with the inner fire that it had kindled.

The tumbling demon vanished. From far down inside the crevice came a crash, and then another and another, echoing remotely. Matt pulled himself back onto the ridge and crawled a few feet; then he made himself stand and walk before he reached the place where the path was broad and safe.

He was battered and bruised, but he could move. Trying to keep in shadow, he limped his way past the phlegmatic, waiting loadbeast. He had gone a dozen steps farther when the two men Nomis had left here as sentries pounced out of deeper shadows. As they seized him his injured leg was twisted again, and he fell.

"Best let me go and run yourselves," he said to the buskined knees standing before him. "Back there, the devil's come for your master."

It made them take a moment to look back toward the distant commotion of injuries and fear. And then they themselves were come for, not by the devil but by the two men Matt had seen running up, axe and sword in hand. Around Matt there swirled a brief clashing of metal, and choked cries that were quickly ended.

"Is this leg your worst hurt, lord?" Harl asked anxiously, putting his axe in his belt and bending over Matt.

"Yes, I do well enough."

Torla muttered grimly: "Then we will go on and slaughter the rest of them."

Matt tried to think. "No. Not now, at least. Nomis called up a thing from the sea——"

Torla shuddered now at the distant moaning. "Then let us away!"

"Can you stand, lord?" asked Harl. "Good, then lean on me." And having pulled Matt to his feet, he next detached something from under his cloak and held it out. "Your helmet, lad. It fell outside the postern gate, and set us on the right trail."

Harl and Torla might think that he was dazed, or that it was pain in his leg that made him so slow to reach out for the helmet. Harl had carried it under his cloak as if it was no more than a shell of metal; but put on like a crown, it weighed enough to crush a man.

Down in the sea-bottom muck the dragon stirred. The tantalizing bait-signal of the life-unit that the Moderns had sent as Ay's replacement was now very near the shore. If that life-unit could be captured without further damage to other life-lines a berserker victory would be insured. To pursue the life-unit inland, among other lives, would involve creating too much change—the dragon's auxiliary man-shaped device might have conducted such a pursuit almost unobtrusively but it had been somehow lost. Still, the chance of seizing the important life-unit right along the coast was too good an opportunity to let slip. Darkening the water with an upheaved cloud of mud, the dragon rose.

Supported by a strong man on either side, Matt could make fair speed along the rough path which led back to Blanium. Not, he thought, that there was any real need for haste. Nomis and his men would certainly not be in pursuit; if Nomis survived at all, his influence would still be thoroughly destroyed.

And the dragon? It had done what it could do to capture him, to take him alive, quietly and gently. He shuddered. It must be hiding in the sea. And it seemed that unless perhaps he went to the water's edge and waved at it, it was not going to chase him. It could have come inland to kill him any time, peasants and armies and the walls of Blanium would not stop it.

No, if the berserker wanted him dead he would be dead

now, and even his magic-sword would not have helped him for a moment. He had seen and heard enough of berserkers to be sure of that.

"How made you your escape, lord?"

"I will tell you later. Let me think, now."

Make the dragon chase you, said Time Ops. We will try to pull you out in time. There had been no pulling-out yet. A king must be ready to give his life, said the Planetary Commander, making what he thought was an important point, if he was speaking from the depths of his own missile-proof shelter.

The Moderns were fighting to save the tribe-of-all-men, and to them Matt or any other individual was only an implement for fighting. Save his life once, then shove him forward again to draw the lightning of the stone-lion's eye. . . .

In a flash of insight, many things suddenly fell into place for Matt. Scraps of knowledge he had picked up in the Moderns' world, about the war as it was fought with screens and missiles, lifelines and keyholes, suddenly dovetailed with what had happened to him here in the world of Ay. Of course, he should have seen it before! It was the Moderns who wanted him killed here, by the berserkers. And the berserkers, knowing this, wanted instead to take him alive!

He was still bleakly pondering this when the communicator in his helmet began to speak into his ear, with its tiny voice that no one else could hear. In his new anger he paid no attention to what it was saying; he came near pulling the helmet off and throwing it away, with all its lying voices. He would throw it away, he told himself, when he came to the sea . . . no, he must avoid the shore from now on. When he came to another bottomless crevice, then.

But instead he gripped his companions' shoulders, stopping them. "Good friends, I must be alone for a little while. To think—and pray."

His good friends exchanged glances with each other; his must seem a strange request, coming at this time. But then their king had been through a day that might make any man act strangely.

Harl frowned at him. "You are weaponless."

"There are no enemies about. But let your dagger stay with me if you will; only let me have a short time to myself."

And so they left him, though with repeated backward glances, left him sitting alone on a rock in the moonlight. He was their king now and they loved him, and he smiled after them with satisfaction, thinking that he would have them at his side for many a year yet. He could and he would. There was no way for the Moderns to punish him, if he chose never to go hunting dragons. Matt was all the Moderns had between themselves and chaos; they would not dare to pull him back to the future, not while he worked at living King Ay's life. He might bungle the job now and then, and provide a second-best defence for the Moderns' world; but it was all the service they were going to get.

He took off the buzzing helmet and scratched his head leisurely. Then, holding the helmet before him, he twisted its right wing, letting Time Ops' tiny voice come out above the faint murmur of the unseen surf.

"—Matt, answer me, it's urgent!"

"I am here. What would you have?"

"Where are you? What's going on?"

"I am going on. To my bride and my kingdom."

There was a pause. Then: "Matt, it may be that won't be enough, your going on trying to take Ay's place."

"No? Enough for me, I think. I have already been demon-hunting, and used up your sword. So I think I will not chase after a dragon that seems content to let me live."

"Demon-hunting? What?"

Matt explained. He could hear consternation at Operations' end; they had not thought of the enemy's trying to capture him alive.

Time Ops was soon back, pleading with a ragged urgency that Matt had never heard in the Commander's voice before. "Matt, whatever else happens, you can't let that thing capture you alive."

"No? I have often been ordered to make it chase me."

"Forget that. No, wait. You can't be captured. But just avoiding capture and going on playing Ay's part isn't going to be good enough, not now. You've done as well as anyone could, but your filling in for Ay just isn't going to work."

"Then why does the enemy want to stop me?"

"Because you *are* buying us a little time here. They want to eliminate any lingering chance we have—any chance of finding

105

some new defence, of pulling off a miracle. They want to play it safe and finish us off quickly. All I can do is tell you—ask you to—go down along the sea shore where the damned thing is hiding, make it come out and chase you and stir up some change."

"And if it should capture me?"

There was a pause, a murmur of voices exchanged at the other end, and then another familiar voice came on.

"Matt, this is Derron. All these people here are trying to figure out the best way to tell you to die. You're to get the berserker to kill you. If it catches you alive, then you find a way to kill yourself. Kill yourself *because* it's caught you. Understand? *Die*, in one way or another, and make the dragon somehow responsible. All along, that's been what Operations wanted of you. I'm sorry. I didn't know how it was, until after you were dropped."

Time Ops came back. "Matt, you can shut us off and go on to your bride and your kingdom, as you said you were going to do. But if you do that, all your life your world there will be slowly decaying around you. Decaying inside where you won't be able to see it, becoming less and less probable. Up here we'll be dying, all of us. At your end of history the chaos will begin in your children's time—that's what you'll be leaving them."

"You lie!" But Matt's voice broke with the cry, for he knew that Time Ops was not lying. Or, if he was lying again about this fact or that, still he was telling the truth about what was needed to win the war. Whatever Time Ops did would be to win the war.

"Matt? This is Derron again. What you just heard is the truth. I don't know what more to say to you."

Matt cried bitterly: "My friend, there is no need for you to say anything more!" And with a jerk of his hand that almost broke the helmet wing, he cut the voices off.

Too late. He had silenced them too late. Slowly he put the helmet back on his head and stood up. Soon he saw Harl and Torla coming toward him; they had doubtless been watching protectively from not far away, overhearing some of the strange language of his prayers.

When they came up to him he said, no longer angry: "My leg gives me trouble. I think the path will be easier along the water's edge."

Between his friends he moved toward the sound of surf. He went slowly, for in truth his leg did feel worse, having stiffened while he sat. No matter, now. He walked along thinking only in disconnected pictures and phrases, since the time for thought and worry was now past.

He had pulled the stone-man from the poison-digger's pit—that was twenty thousand years ago, and indeed it seemed to him that he had lived through twenty thousand years since then. He had been able to see the tribe-of-all-men grown to stretch across immensities of space and time. He had known, a little, the spirits of life. He had been a king, and a woman with the spirit of a princess had looked at him with love.

They had been walking for a minute along the water's edge, when without surprise he saw a shoreline rock ahead suddenly move, to become a nightmare head that rose amid moonlit spray on a sinuous column of neck. The dragon's vast body heaved itself up from the sea, and lurched toward the men faster than a man could run.

"I have the dagger," Matt said to his friends. "And right now both of you can use sword and axe better than I." The dragon was not coming for Harl or Torla, and anyway it would be a pointless insult to bid them run.

He kept the dagger hidden in his hand, the blade turned up flat behind his wrist, as the dragon's head came straight for him on its tree-trunk neck that could swallow a man and hold him safe. Sword and axe hewed uselessly from either side. Matt was very tired, and in a way he welcomed the grave-wide jaws, which he saw now held no teeth. Only in the instant of the jaws' soft powerful closing did he bring the dagger up, holding the point steady at his own heart while the pressure came down. . . .

"It killed him." The first time, Time Ops whispered the words unbelievingly. Then he let them out in a whoop. "It killed him, it killed him!" The other hunters who had been frozen at their screens, sharing their computers' creeping certainty of failure, were galvanized once more into action. On their screens the spiderwebs tightened like nooses, imaging a target greenly solid and sure.

In the deep cave called Operations Stage Two, metallic arms extended a missile sideways from its rack while a silvery circle shimmered into being on the floor beneath. With a click and a jolt the arms released their burden. Falling, the missile was gone——

Derron had seen a keyhole hit and closed before, and he understood perfectly what a victory he was seeing now. On the screens, the whole writhing build-up of change surrounding Ay now burst like a boil, began to straighten itself out like a piece of trickery with string. History's flow turned strongly and safely back into the familiar riverbed. Only the one lifeline that had been the catalyst was newly broken; you had to look closely at the screens not to miss that small detail.

The raw stump of that line left no room for reasonable doubt, but still Derron's hand went out to punch his communicator for Stage Three. "Alf? Listen, will you let me know what shape he's in, the moment—all right, thanks."

He waited, holding the circuit open to Stage Three, gazing blankly through tired eyes at the screens. Around him in Operations' nerve centre the first waves of a celebration curled up around the edges of discipline.

"Derron?" Alf's voice was slow in coming, and slow-spoken when it came, to tell about the knife in the heart and speculate on how the man must have arranged to have it driven there. And to confirm that Matt's brain had been too long without blood and oxygen for the medics to do anything for him now.

Derron flipped off the switch and sat at his post, tired and immobile. Some of the victorious hunters around him were breaking out cigars, and one was calling jovially for a ration of grog. A few minutes later Time Ops himself came strolling by with a glass in his hand, but he was not shouting or even smiling as he paused at Derron's position.

"He was a good man, Odegard. The best, of course. Not many can accomplish a thousandth part of what he did. With their lives or with their deaths." Time Ops raised his glass in a solemn sipping toast to the bitten-off green line on the screen. Later, of course, there would be ceremonies and monuments to do the same thing more elaborately.

"The thing is," said Derron, "I don't really care much what happens to the world. Only about a person here and there."

Time Ops might not have heard, for the celebration was growing louder. "You did a necessary job, major, and did it well, from the start of the operation until today. We're going to be expanding even more here in Time Operations, and we'll need good men in key positions. I'm going to recommend you for another promotion. . . ."

Nomis stood with arms upraised, grey beard and black robes whipping in the wind, while he persisted in the evil endeavour that had kept him here for the past three days on his secret pinnacle of rock. Nomis persisted, though he could not escape the feeling that his labours against Ay were doomed to be all in vain. . . .

On the battlement, Alix shaded her eyes against the morning sun, and strained them seaward to catch sight of sail or mast. She waited, trembling inwardly a little, for her first sight of her future husband and lord. . . .

The cliffs of Queensland were dead ahead, Harl knew, though still a day's rowing out of sight. He frowned to port, gazing out across the sea's grey face, though there was nothing to break the line of the horizon but a distant line of squalls. Then his face cleared with the thought that young Ay, in his tent amidships, was doubtless planning for the fighting that was sure to come.

PART THREE

The barefoot man in the grey friar's habit topped a rise and paused, taking a look at the country ahead of him. In that direction, the paved road he was following continued to run almost straight under a leaden sky, humping over one gentle hill after another, cutting scrubby woods and untended fields. The stones of this road had been laid down in the days of glory of the great Continental Empire, and there was not much else in the world that had survived the centuries between then and now.

From where the friar stood, the road appeared to be aimed at a slender tower, a sharp and lonely temple-spire, grey and vague with the day's dull light, which rose from an unseen base at some miles' distance. The friar had walked with that spire in sight for half a day already, but his goal lay far beyond.

The friar was of medium height, and wiry build. His appearance seemed to have little to do with his age, which might have been anywhere between twenty and forty. His scantily-bearded face was tired now, and his grey robe was spotted with greyer mud. The fields here along the shoulders of the road were all ankle-deep in mud, and showed no sign of having been ploughed or planted this spring or last.

"Oh Holy One, I thank You again that I have had this pavement to follow for so much of my journey," the friar murmured, as he started forward again. His feet looked scarred and tough as well-used hiking boots.

Excepting the distant spire, the only sign of any recent human presence in this unpromising landscape was a heap of low ruined walls at the roadside just ahead. Only the fact of ruin was recent; the walls themselves were old and might have been a part of a caravanserai or military post in the days of the Empire's strength. But last month or last tenday a new war had passed this way, dissolving one more building into raw tumbled stones. What was left of the structure looked as if it might be going to sink without a trace into the mud, before even the spring grass could start to grow on it.

The friar sat down on the remnant of the wall when he reached it, resting from his long journey and looking with minor sadness at the minor destruction about him. After a bit, like a man who has trouble keeping entirely still, he leaned over and picked up one of the fallen stones, in lean hands that showed a strength. Looking at the stone with what might have been a practised mason's eye, he fitted it deftly into a notch in the stump of wall, and sat back to study the effect.

A distant hail made him raise his head and look back along the way he had come. Another lone figure, dressed in a habit much like his own, was hastening toward him, waving both arms for attention.

The first friar's thin face lighted gently at the prospect of company. He returned the wave and waited, forgetting his little game of masonry. Soon he got to his feet.

Presently the approaching figure resolved itself into a man of middle height, who was almost stout and who had recently been clean-shaven. "Glory to the Holy One, reverend brother!" puffed this newcomer, as he arrived at last within easy talking distance.

"Glory to His name." The bearded friar's voice was warm but unremarkable.

The portly one, a man of about thirty, seated himself on the low wall, wiped at his face, puffed, and inquired anxiously: "Are you, as I think, Brother Jovann of Ernard?"

"That is my name."

"Now may the Holy One be praised!" The heavier man made a wedge-sign with his hands, and rolled his eyes heavenward. "My name is Saile, brother. Now may the Holy One be praised, say I——"

"So be it."

"——for He has led me in mysterious ways to reach your side! And many more shall follow. Brother Jovann, men will flock to you from the four corners of the world, for the fame of your heroic virtue has spread far, to the land of Mosnar, or so I have heard, and to the lands of the Infidel even. And here in our own land—even at this moment, in the isolated villages of these remote hills, some of the most backward peasants are aware of your passage."

"I fear my many faults are known hereabouts, for I was born not far away."

"Ah, Brother Jovann, you are overly modest. During my arduous struggles to reach your side I have heard again and again of your holy exploits."

Brother Jovann, showing some concern, sat down on the wall again. "Why have you struggled, as you say, to reach my side?"

"Ahh." What a struggle it had been, said Saile's headshake. "The flame of my determination was first kindled several months ago, when I was told by unimpeachable sources, eye-witnesses, how, when you were with the army of the Faithful in the field, you dared to leave the sheltering ranks, to cross no-man's-land into the very jaws of the infidel; there to enter the tent of the Arch-Infidel himself and preach to him the truth of our Holy Temple!"

"And to fail to convert him." Jovann nodded sadly. "You do well to remind me of my failure, for I am prone to the sin of pride."

"Ah." Saile lost headway, but only for a moment. "It was, as I say, upon hearing of that exploit, Brother Jovann, that it became my own most humble wish, my most burning and holy ambition, to seek you out, to be among the very first to join your order." Saile's eyebrows went up questioningly. "Ah, it is true then, that you *are* even now on your way to Empire City, to petition our most holy Vicar Nabur for permission to found a new religious order?"

The thin friar's eyes looked toward the spire in the distance. "Once, brother, God called me to rebuild fallen temples with stone and brick—now, as you say, I am called to rebuild with men." His attention came back, smiling, to Brother Saile. "As for your becoming a member of the new order when it is formed, why I can say nothing yet of that. But if you should choose to walk with me to Empire City, I will be happy for your company."

Saile jumped to his feet, to bob up and down with bowing. "It is I who am most happy and most honoured, Brother Jovann!"

Saile prolonged his thanks as the two men walked on together. He had also commented at some length on the unpleasant prospect of yet more rain falling, and was discoursing on the problem of where in this deserted-looking land two mendicant friars might hope to obtain their next meal, when there occurred a distraction.

A speedy coach was overtaking them on the road. The vehicle was not ornate but was well-built, looking as if it might belong to some nobleman or prelate of lower-middle rank. The friars' ears gave them plenty of warning to step aside; four agile loadbeasts were making the wheels clatter over the levelled stones at a good speed.

As the coach rumbled past, Brother Jovann found his eyes drawn to the face of an occupant who rode facing forward, his head and one elbow extended slightly from a window. So far as could be judged, this man was stocky of build. He was well-dressed, old and grey-bearded, though the short-cut hair atop his head was still of a ginger colour. His thick mouth was twisted slightly, as if ready to spit or to dispute.

"They might have given us a lift," Brother Saile muttered unhappily, looking after the coach as it dwindled into the distance. "Plenty of room. There were no more than two passengers, were there?"

Brother Jovann shook his head, not having noticed if there were other passengers or not. His attention had been held by the old man's eyes, which had probably never seen the friars at all. Those eyes, fixed in the direction of the Holy City a hundred miles and more away, were clear and grey and powerful. But they were also very much afraid.

When Derron Odegard walked out on the victory celebration in Time Operations he had no clear idea of where he was going. Only when he found himself approaching the nearby hospital complex did he realize that his feet were taking him to Lisa. Yes, it would be best to face her at once and get it over with.

At the Student Nurses' quarters he learned that she had moved out the day before, after having got approval to drop out of training there. While being tested and considered for other jobs she was sharing a cubicle with another girl in a low-rank uplevel corridor.

There, it was Lisa's new room-mate who opened the door to Derron's knock; since the girl was in the midst of doing something to her hair, she then had to go back inside and pretend not to be listening.

Lisa must have seen Derron's news in his face. Her own face at once became as calm as a mask, and she remained just inside the half-open door, letting him stand in the narrow corridor to be brushed by the curious and incurious passers-by.

"It's Matt," he said to her. When there was no reaction, he went on: "Oh, the battle's won, the berserkers are stopped. But he sacrificed himself to do it. He's dead."

Proud and hard as a shield, her mask-face lifted slightly toward him. "Of course he is. He did the job you gave him. I knew he would."

"Understand, Lisa, when I went to him with that sales-talk I thought he was going to have a chance, a good chance."

She was not going to be able to keep the shield up after all; with something like relief he saw her face begin to move and heard her voice begin to break. She said: "I—knew you were going to kill him."

"My God, Lisa, that wasn't what I meant to do!" He kept his hands from reaching out to her.

Slowly dissolving and melting into a woman's grief, she leaned against the doorjamb, her hands hidden behind her. "And now—there's—n-nothing to be done!"

"The doctors tried—but no, nothing. And Operations can't go back to do anything for Matt in the past—it'd wreck the world to try to pull him out of that mess now."

"The world's not worth it!"

He was murmuring some banality and reaching out at last to try to comfort her, when the door slammed in his face.

Of course if Lisa was the woman he needed he would have stayed there; so he thought to himself a few days later as he sat alone in his tiny private office on the Operations' level. He would have stayed and made her open the door again, or kicked it down. It was only a door of plastic, and behind it she was still alive.

The fact was, of course, that the woman he did need had been for a year and more behind the door of death. And no man could smash through that. A man could only stand before that door and mourn, until he found that he was able to turn away.

Derron had been sitting in his office staring into space for some little time before he noticed an official-looking envelope that some courier must have left on his small desk. The envelope was neat and thick, sealed and addressed to him. After looking inertly at it for a while he took it up and opened it.

Inside was the formal notice of his latest promotion, to the rank of lieutenant colonel "—in consideration of your recent outstanding service in Time Operations, and in the expectation that you will continue——" A set of appropriate collar insignia were enclosed.

The insignia held in his hand as if forgotten, he sat there a while longer, looking across the room at an object—it was an ancient battle-helmet, ornamented with wings—that rested like a trophy atop his small bookcase. He was still doing this when the clangour of the alert signal sounded throughout Operations and pulled him reflexively to his feet. In another moment he was out of the door and on his way to the briefing room.

Latecomers were still hurrying in when a general officer, Time Ops' chief of staff, mounted the dais and began to speak.

"The third assault we've been expecting has begun, gentlemen. Win or lose, this will be the last attack the berserkers can mount outside of present-time. It'll give us the final bearing we need to locate their staging area twenty-one thousand years down."

There were a few scattered expressions of optimism.

"I suggest that you don't cheer yet. This third attack gives every indication of involving some new tactics on the enemy's part, something subtle and extremely dangerous."

The general performed the usual unveiling of some hastily assembled maps and models. "Like the previous attack, this one is aimed at a single individual; and, again, there's no doubt about the target's identity. This time the name is Vincento Vincento."

There was a murmur at that name, a ripple of awe and wonder and concern. There would have been a similar reaction from almost any audience that might have been assembled on Sirgol. Even the half-educated of that world had heard of Vincento, though the man was some three hundred years dead and had never ruled a nation, started a religion, or raised an army.

Derron's attention became sharply focused, and he sat up straighter, his feeling of inertia slipping away. In his pre-war historical studies he had specialized in Vincento's time and place—and that locale was also oddly connected with his private grief.

The general on the dais spoke on, in business-like tones. "Vincento's lifeline is among the very few ultra-important ones for which we have provided continuous sentry protection along their entire effective lengths. Of course this doesn't mean that a berserker can't get near him. But should one of them try to do violent harm to Vincento, or even to any other person within a couple of miles of him, we'd be onto its keyhole in a couple of seconds and cancel it out. The same thing applies if they should try to kidnap or capture Vincento himself.

"This special protection actually starts back in Vincento's grandparents' time, and runs along his lifeline until his completion of his last important work at the age of seventy-eight, and we can assume the enemy knows that this protection exists. That's why I said that this time the berserkers' plans are no doubt subtle."

After going into the technical details of the sentry-protection against direct violence, the general moved on to discuss another point. "Chronologically, the enemy penetration is not more than a tenday before the start of Vincento's famous trial by the Defenders of the Faith. This may well be more than a coincidence. Suppose for example that a berserker could alter the outcome of this trial to a death sentence for Vincento. If the Defenders should decide to burn him at the stake, the berserker's part in his death would be too indirect to give us any help in finding its keyhole.

"And remember, too, an actual death sentence would not seem to be necessary for the enemy's purpose. Vincento at the time of his trial is seventy years old. If he should be put to torture or thrown into a dungeon, the odds are high that his life would be effectively ended."

A general seated in the front row raised a hand. "Doesn't he historically undergo some such treatment?"

"No. That's a fairly common idea. But historically, Vincento never spent a day of his life in prison. During his trial he occupied a friendly ambassador's quarters. And after his recantation, he passed the few years left to him in physically comfortable house arrest. There he gradually went blind, from natural causes—and also laid the foundation of the science of dynamics. On that work of his, needless to say, our modern science and our survival most heavily depend. Make no mistake about it, those last years of Vincento's life after his trial are vital to us."

The questioning general shifted in his front rank chair. "How in the world is an alien machine going to influence the outcome of a trial in an ecclesiastical court?"

The briefing officer could only shake his head, and stare gloomily at his charts. "Frankly, we've still a shortage of good ideas on that. We doubt that the enemy will try again to play a supernatural role, after the failure of their last attempt along that line.

"But here's an angle worth keeping in mind. Only one enemy device is engaged in this attack, and from all screen indications it's a physically small machine, only about the size of a man. Which immediately suggests to us the possibility that this one may be an android." The speaker paused to look round at his audience. "Oh yes, I know, the berserkers have never, anywhere, been able to fabricate an android that would pass in human society as a normal person. Still we hardly dare rule out the possibility that this time they've succeeded."

A discussion got going on possible countermeasures. A whole arsenal of devices were being kept in readiness in Stage Two for dropping into the past, but no one could say yet what might be needed.

The briefing officer pushed his charts aside for the moment. "The one really bright spot, of course, is that this attack lies within the time band where we can drop live agents. So naturally we'll count on putting men on the spot as our main defence. Their job will be to keep their eyes on Vincento from a little distance; they'll be people able to spot any significant deviation from history when they see it. Those we choose as agents will need to know that particular period very well, besides having experience in Time Operations . . ."

Listening, Derron looked down at the new insignia he was still carrying in his hand. And then he began at last to fasten them on.

118

About two miles along the road from the spot where they had met, Brother Jovann and Brother Saile topped yet another rise and discovered that they were about to catch up with the coach that had passed them so speedily not long before. Its loadbeasts unharnessed and grazing nearby, the vehicle stood empty beside the broken gate of a high-walled enclosure which crouched under slate roofs at the foot of the next hill ahead.

Atop that hill there rose the already famed cathedral-temple of Oibbog, much of its stonework still too new to bear moss or signs of weathering. Holding its spire now immense and over-shadowing against the lowering sky, the graceful mass seemed almost to float, secure above all human effort and concern.

The ancient road, after passing the broken-gated monastery at the foot of the new cathedral's hill, swerved left to meet a bridge. Or the stub of a bridge, rather. From where the friars now stood they could see that all of the spans were gone, together with four of the six piers that had supported them. The river that had torn them down was raging still, jamming treetrunks like forked spears against the supports that remained. Obviously swollen to several times its normal flow, the current was ravaging the lowlands on both its banks.

On the other side of the torrent, beyond another stub of bridge, the walled town of Oibbog sat on its secure high ground. People could be seen moving here and there in those distant streets. Inside the town's gate that opened on the Empire road, more coaches and loadbeasts waited, having been interrupted in journeys outbound from the Holy City.

Brother Jovann watched leaden clouds still mounting ominously up the sky. Fleeing from these clouds was the river, a great swollen terrified snake being lashed and goaded by distant flails of lightning, a snake that had burst its bonds and carried them away.

"Brother River will not let us cross tonight."

When he heard this personification, Brother Saile turned his head slowly and cautiously around, as if he wondered whether he was expected to laugh. But before he had to decide the rain broke again, like a waterfall. Tucking up the skirts of their robes, both friars ran. Jovann sprinted barefoot, Saile with sandals flapping, to join the occupants of the coach in whatever shelter the abandoned-looking monastery might afford.

A hundred miles away, in what had been the capital of the vanished Empire and was now the Holy City of the embattled Temple, the same day was warm and sultry. Only the wrath of Nabur the Eighth, eighty-first in the succession of Vicars of the Holy One, stirred like a storm-wind the air of his luxurious private apartments.

This wrath had been some time accumulating, thought Defender Belam, who stood in robes of princely scarlet, waiting in silent gravity for it to be over. It had been accumulated and saved till now when it could be discharged harmlessly, vented into the discreet ears of a most trusted auditor and friend.

The Vicar's peripatetic tirade against his military and theological opponents broke off in mid-sentence; Nabur was distracted and his pacing stopped by a dull scraping sound, ending in a heavy thud, which floated in from outside, accompanied by the shouts of workmen. The Vicar moved to look down from a balconied window into a courtyard. Earlier, Belam had seen the workmen down there, starting to unload some massive blocks of marble from a train of carts. Today a famed sculptor was to choose one block, and begin work on Nabur's portrait-statue.

What did it matter if each of eighty predecessors had been willing to let their worldly glorification wait upon posterity?

The Vicar turned from the balcony suddenly, the skirts of his simple white robe swirling, and caught Belam wearing a disapproving face.

In his angry tenor, that had for the past forty years sounded like an old man's voice, the Vicar declaimed: "When the statue is completed we will have it placed in the city's Great Square, that the majesty of our office and our person may be increased in the eyes of the people!"

"Yes, my Vicar." Belam's tone was quite calm. For decades he had been a Defender of the Faith and a Prince of the Temple. From close range he had seen them come and go, and he was not easily perturbed by Vicarial tempers.

Nabur felt the need to explain. "Belam, it is *needful* that we be shown increased respect. The infidels and heretics are tearing apart the world which has been given by God into our care!" The last sentence came bursting out, a cry from the inner heart.

"My faith is firm, my Vicar, that our prayers and our armies will yet prevail."

"Prevail?" The Vicar came stalking toward him, grimacing sarcastically. "Of course! Someday. Before the end of time! But *now*, Belam, *now* our Holy Temple lies bleeding and suffering, and we . . ." The Vicarial voice dropped temporarily into almost inaudible weakness. "We must bear many burdens. Many and heavy, Belam. You cannot begin to realize, until you mount our throne."

Belam bowed, in sincere and silent reverence.

The Vicar paced again, skirts flapping. This time he had a goal. From his high-piled worktable he snatched up in shaking fist a pamphlet that was already worn from handling, and wrinkled as if it had perhaps been once or twice crumpled up and thrown across a room.

Belam knew what the pamphlet was. A contributing if not a sufficient cause of today's rage, he thought, in his cool habit of theologian's logic. A small thorn compared with others. But this particular barb had stabbed Nabur in the tenderest part of his vanity.

Nabur was shaking the paper-covered booklet at him. "Because you have been away, Belam, we have not yet had the opportunity to discuss with you this—this back-stabbing abomination of Messire Vincento's! This so-called *Dialogue On The Movement Of The Tides*! Have you read it?"

"I——"

"The wretched man cares nothing about the tides. In this pamphlet his purpose is to once more promulgate his heresy-tainted dreams. He clings to his wish to reduce the solid world beneath our feet to a mere speck, to send us all flying round the sun. But even that is not enough. No, not for him!"

Belam frowned now in real puzzlement. "What else, my Vicar?"

Nabur advanced on him in a glow of anger, as if the Defender were the guilty one. "What else? I will tell you! The arguments of this pamphlet are cast in the form of a debate among three persons. And Vincento its author intends one of these fictional debaters—the one who defends traditional ideas, who therefore is described as 'simple-minded' and 'below the level of human intelligence'—he intends this person to represent ourself!"

"My Vicar!"

Nabur nodded vigorously. "Oh yes. Some of our very words are put into the mouth of this simpleton, so-called!"

Belam was shaking his head in strong doubt. "Vincento has never been moderate in his disputes, which have been many. Many? Nay, continuous, rather. But I am convinced that he has not in this pamphlet or elsewhere intended any irreverence, either to your person or to your holy office."

"I know what he intended here!" Vicar Nabur almost screamed the words. Then the most honoured man in the world—possibly also the most hated, quite possibly also the most burdened by what he saw as his God-given tasks—groaned incontinently, and like a spoiled child threw himself into a chair.

Arrogance remained, as always, but the spoiled-child aspect did not last long. Irascible humours having been discharged, calm and intelligence returned.

"Belam."

"My Vicar?"

"Have you yet had time to study this pamphlet, while on your travels perhaps? I know it has been widely circulated."

Belam gravely inclined his head.

"Then give us your considered opinion."

"I am a theologian, my Vicar, and not a natural philosopher. Therefore I have taken counsel with astronomers and others, and find my own opinion in this matter generally confirmed. Which is that Vincento's arguments in this pamphlet concerning the tides really prove nothing regarding the movement of the celestial bodies, and are not even very accurate as regards the tides themselves."

"He thinks we are all fools, to be dazzled by brilliant words into accepting whatever shoddy logic he offers us. And that we will not even realize it when we are mocked!" The Vicar stood up for a moment, sighed, and then tiredly resumed his seat.

Belam chose to ignore the theory, which he did not for a moment believe, that the pamphlet's aim was sacrilegious mockery. The real issue was vital enough. "As the Vicar may possibly recall, I had occasion some years ago to write to Vincento regarding his speculations on the idea of a sun-centred universe. Then, as now, such theorizing caused me concern in my capacity as Defender."

"We recall the occasion very well, ha hum. In fact Messire Vincento has already been summoned here to stand trial, for his violation in this pamphlet of your injunction at that time ... Belam, what were the precise words of your warning, again?"

Belam thought awhile before answering, and then spoke slowly and precisely. "I wrote him, first, that mathematicians are quite free to calculate and publish whatever they wish regarding the celestial appearances or any other natural phenomena—provided they remain strictly in the realm of hypothesis.

"Secondly, it is quite a different matter to say that *in fact* the sun is in the centre of the universe. That *in fact* our globe spins from west to east each day, while revolving round the sun each year. Such statements must be considered very dangerous; though not formally heretical, they are liable to injure faith by contradicting the Holy Writings."

"Your memory, Belam, is even more than usually excellent. Just when did you write this letter of injunction?"

"Fifteen years ago, my Vicar." Belam showed a dry smile momentarily. "Though I must admit that I re-read our archive copy this morning."

He was utterly serious again. "Thirdly and lastly, I wrote Vincento that if some real proof existed of the sun-centred universe he champions, we should then be forced to revise our interpretations of those passages in the Holy Writings which would appear to say otherwise. We have in the past revised our Scriptural interpretations, for example in regard to the roundness of the world. But, in the absence of any such proof, the weight of authority and traditional opinion is not to be set aside."

Nabur was listening with great attentiveness. "It seems to us, Belam, that you wrote well, as usual."

"Thank you, my Vicar."

Satisfaction appeared mixed with anger in the Vicarial mien. "Certainly in this pamphlet Vincento has violated your injunction! The debater into whose mouth he puts his own opinions advances no convincing proofs, at least none that can be grasped by mere mortals like ourselves. And yet he does argue, at great length, that in very truth our globe spins like a toy top beneath our feet. To convince the reader of this is his plain intention. Then!" The Vicar stood up, dramatically.

"Then on the last page *our* argument—often expressed by us as a means of compromising these difficult philosophical matters—*our* argument, that God may produce whatever effect He likes in the world, without being bound by scientific causes —*our* argument is quoted by the simpleton-debater who has been wrong about everything else; quoted as coming from 'a person of high learning and wisdom, supremely above contradiction'. And at this the other debaters piously declare themselves silenced, and decide to adjourn for refreshment. One cannot fail to see them, and their author, laughing up their sleeves!"

While the Vicar struggled to once more regain his breath and calm there was silence in the apartment, save for the workmen's shouts and laughter drifting in. What were they doing out there? Oh yes, only the marble. Belam uttered a brief prayer that he might never again be required to order a stake prepared for a heretic.

When Nabur spoke again, it was in a reasonable tone. "Now, Belam. Other than this weary argument on tides, which all seem to agree is inconclusive, do you suppose there can exist anywhere any evidence for Vincento's spinning world? Anything he might impertinently introduce at his trial, to . . . disrupt its course?"

Belam drew himself up, slightly but perceptibly. "My Vicar, we shall of course conduct Vincento's trial, or any other, with the greatest zeal for the truth that we can muster. Vincento of course may argue in his own defence——"

"Of course, of course!" Nabur interrupted with a rapid dismissive waving of his hand; it was the gesture he used when another man might apologize. But then he still waited for an answer.

After frowning thoughtfully at the floor, Belam began to give what a later age would call a background briefing. "My Vicar, I have through the years made an effort to keep abreast of astronomers' thinking. I fear many of them, religious and laymen both, have become Messire Vincento's enemies. He has a relish and skill for making others look like fools. He has arrogance, in claiming for his own all that these new devices, telescopes, discover in the heavens. An arrogant and argumentative man is hard to bear, and triply hard when he is so often in the right." Belam glanced up sharply for a moment, but Nabur had not taken the description as applying to anyone but Vincento. "My Vicar, is it not true that this pamphlet was brought to your attention by some priest-astronomer whom Vincento has offended, and bested in some debate?" Though Belam knew of a number of such men, he was really only guessing.

"Hum. It may be so, Belam, it may be so. But Vincento's offence is real, though it may have been maliciously called to our attention."

The two of them were pacing now, with old men's measured treads, sometimes orbiting each other like perturbed planets. The Defender of the Faith said: "I raise the point to show the difficulty of obtaining unbiased testimony in this matter from other scholars. They are certainly unlikely to rush to Vincento's defence. Nevertheless, I believe that most astronomers now perform their calculations using the mathematical assumption that the planets, or some of them at least, revolve about the sun. Of course that idea is not original with Vincento, nor is the idea that our globe is only a planet. It seems these assumptions make the mathematics of celestial movement more elegant and somewhat more satisfying to the scholar; fewer epicycles need be included in the orbits to make them fit the circular form——"

"Yes, yes. Vincento makes the mathematics more elegant. But stick to the point. Can he have *proof,* mathematical or otherwise? Plain evidence of any kind?"

"I would say rather the contrary."

"Ha!" Nabur stopped pacing and faced Belam squarely, almost smiling.

The Defender said: "Had Vincento any plain proof, I think he would have printed it here. And there *is* solid evidence against him." Belam gestured with his scholar's hands, frail fingers unsure of technicalities but still grasping firmly whatever they were required to grasp. "It seems that if our globe did make a yearly journey round the sun, the relative positions of the fixed stars should appear to us to change from month to month, as we approached certain constellations or drew away from them. And no such displacement of the stars can be observed."

Vicar Nabur was nodding, looking satisfied.

Belam made a shrugging gesture. "Of course it is possible to argue that the stars are simply too distant for our measurements to discover such displacement. Vincento will always have arguments, if he wants to use them . . . I fear that no other astronomer is going to be able to prove him wrong, much as some of them would love to do so. No, I think we must admit that the celestial appearances would be essentially the same if we *did* go round the sun."

"That is enough for any reasonable man to say."

"Exactly, my Vicar. As I wrote Vincento, where there is lack of other certainty, we have no excuse for turning our backs on tradition and substituting strained interpretations for the plain meaning of the Holy Writings." Belam's voice was rising gradually, achieving the tone of power that it would have in court. "We of the Temple have the solemn duty before God to uphold the truth that those Writings reveal. And, my Vicar, what I wrote to Vincento fifteen years ago is still true today—I have never been shown any proof of the motion of the world we stand on, and so I cannot believe that any such proof or any such motion exists!"

The Vicar had resumed his seat. Now his face was gentle, as he raised his hands, then clamped them down decisively on the arms of his ornate work-chair. "Then it is our decision that you and the other Defenders must proceed with the trial." Nabur spoke regretfully at first, though as he went on his anger gradually returned, less vehement than it had been. "We do not doubt that he can be convicted of violating your injunction. But understand, we have no wish to visit any great punishment upon our erring son."

Belam bowed his grateful assent to that.

Nabur went on: "In charity we grant that he intended no attack upon the Faith, and no insult to our person. He is only headstrong, and stubborn, and intemperate in debate. And sadly lacking in gratitude, and humility! He must be taught that he *cannot* set himself up as a superior authority on all matters temporal and spiritual . . . did he not once attempt to lecture *you* on theology?"

Belam once more inclined his head in assent, meanwhile sharply warning himself that he must guard against taking any personal satisfaction in Vincento's approaching humiliation.

Even now Nabur could not let the subject drop, not yet. "Ah, I could curse the man! In the past, we ourself have been among the first to heap praise on his achievements. We have granted him hours of private audience. We have shown him friendliness to a degree we do not always extend to princes! Before ascending to this chair, we ourself once even wrote a pamphlet in his praise! And now, how are we repaid?"

"I understand, my Vicar."

"I see you have requested assignment to one particular time, Colonel Odegard." Colonel Lukas spoke the words around his cigar, while at the same time using the formal style of address. He was a sometime drinking acquaintance of Derron's who might be finding it a little difficult to strike the right balance in his role today of examining psychologist. If he had been a close friend of Derron's he would probably have disqualified himself as examiner. But what close friends did Derron have these days among the living? There was Chan Amling . . . an old classmate, yes. Bosom buddy, no. The fact was that he had none.

Lukas was looking at him. "Yes, I did," Derron answered, somewhat tardily.

Lukas shifted his cigar. "The two days Vincento spends near the town of Oibbog, delayed on his way to his trial. Waiting to cross a flooded river. Had you any particular reason for wanting that time?"

Oh yes, he had. He had not put it into words, however, even for himself, and was not about to try to do so now. "Just that I know the locale very well. I once spent a long holiday there. It was one of those places that didn't change very much in three or four hundred years." Of course the town and cathedral of Oibbog, like all the other surface landmarks of the planet, were now in the past tense. Derron's particular reason was that the long holiday there had been with *her*. He caught himself sliding forward tensely on his chair again, and forced himself to slump a little and relax.

Squinting through his cigar smoke, Colonel Lukas shuffled uncertainly through the papers on his desk, and then threw one of his sneaky fast-balls. "Have you any particular reason for wanting to be an agent at all?"

For Derron that question immediately called up an image of Matt and Ay, two forms blending more and more into a single kingly figure as they receded from the moving moment of the present. Their heroic image seemed to be growing steadily larger with distance, the way a mountain in the old days on the surface had sometimes seemed to swell as you hiked away from it.

But that was not the sort of reason a man could talk about; at least not without all of a sudden sounding far too noble and dedicated.

Derron made himself slide back in his chair again. "Well, as I said, I know the period very well. I believe I can do a good job. Like everyone else, I want to win the war." He was uttering noble sentiments after all, and too many of them. Better stretch it into a joke. "I want prestige, I suppose. Accomplishment. Promotion. You name it. Did I hit the right one yet?"

"What is the right one?" Lukas shrugged glumly. "I don't know why I'm required to ask that—why does anyone want to be an agent?" He shaped his papers into a neat stack before him. "Now, colonel. Just one more thing I want to bring up before certifying you as good agent material. That is the matter of your personal religious views."

"I'm not religious."

"How do you feel *about* religion?"

Relax, relax. "Well, frankly, I think that gods and temples are fine things for people who need crutches. I haven't yet found any necessary."

"I see. I think this is a valid psychological point which should be raised, because there are dangers inherent in sending back to Vincento's time anyone who is likely to find himself susceptible to ideological fever." Lukas made an apologetic gesture. "You as an historian understand better than I how thick dogmas and doctrines are in the air back there. Religious and philosophical controversy seems to draw all the energy of that era."

"Yes." Derron nodded. "I see what you mean. You don't want a fanatic of any stripe. Well, I'm not what they call a militant atheist. My conscience will let me play any part that's necessary." Maybe he was explaining too much, talking too much, but he had to make this point, he had to be allowed to go. "I'll be a rabid monk and spit on Vincento if required."

"I don't suppose Time Ops will ask that of you. All right, then, Derron. You're in."

And Derron tried not to show too much relief.

What Operations really decided was that he would do best in the part of a travelling scholar. They gave him a name—Valzay—and started to build for him an identity that had never historically existed. He was supposedly from Mosnar, a country distant from Vincento's but for the most part faithful to the Holy Temple. Valzay was to be one of the itinerant intellectuals of Vincento's time, who wandered somewhat like sacred cows across minor political and language boundaries, from one university or wealthy patron to another.

Derron and a dozen other chosen agents, mostly male, were rushed into preparation. Working singly or in pairs, they were to keep Vincento under practically continuous observation during the now doubly critical days of his life just preceding his trial and during it. Each agent or team would remain on the job for a day or two and then be relieved by another. Chan Amling, now a captain, was assigned as Derron's team partner; they would not be much together on the job, but would alternate in keeping Vincento more or less in sight. Amling was to play the role of one of the wandering friars who in Vincento's day were quite numerous, and for the most part only loosely disciplined.

The programme of preparation was hurried and rugged, beginning with the surgical implantation of communications transducers in jawbone and skull. This would enable each agent to remain in contact with Operations without having to mumble aloud, or wear anything as bulky as a helmet.

There were speech and manners to be rehearsed, some knowledge of events current in Vincento's day to be memorized, and some knowledge to be repressed, of events in the immediate future of that time. There were the techniques of communications and weaponry to be mastered—all this in a few days.

Amid his fatigue and concentration Derron noticed almost without surprise that Lisa was now working in Operations, one of the calm-voiced girls who relayed orders and information to individual sentries and could do the same for slave-unit operators, or for live agents when some of them took the field.

He had only scraps of free time now, and made no effort to use any of it to speak to her. The knowledge that he was on his way back to Oibbog had crowded almost everything else out of his mind. He felt like a man going to a rendezvous with his own true love; the people of flesh and blood around him, Lisa included, took on the semblance of shadows for him and even as the dead past grew more vivid.

Then one day as he and Amling sat in folding chairs at the side of Stage Three, resting between behaviour drills, Lisa came walking past, and stopped.

"Derron, I want to wish you success."

"Thanks. Pull up a chair, if you like."

She did. Amling decided he wanted to stretch his legs, and ambled away.

Lisa said: "Derron, I shouldn't have accused you of killing Matt. I know you didn't want him to die, that you felt as bad as I did about it. What happened to him wasn't your fault." She was speaking like someone who had lost a friend among other friends in war. Not like someone whose life had been destroyed with the life of her beloved. "I've just been mastering my own internal difficulties—you know about that—but that's no excuse for what I said. I should have known you better. I'm sorry."

"It's all right." Derron shifted uncomfortably in his chair, sorry that she felt so bad about it. "Really, it's ... Lisa, I thought you and I might have had—something. I suppose not the whole thing there can be between a man and a woman, but still something good."

She looked away from him, a faint frown creasing her forehead. "I had some feeling like that about Matt. But that much of a feeling would never be enough for me."

He went on hurriedly: "As far as anything permanent and tremendous is concerned, well, I've tried that already, once in my life. And I'm still up to my neck in it, as you may have noticed. I'm sorry, I've got to get moving." And he jumped up out of his chair and hurried to where Amling and the others were not yet ready for him.

When the day came for the drop, the costumiers dressed Derron in clothing that was slightly worn but good, suitable for a fairly successful gentleman-scholar on his travels far from home. In his haversack they placed a reasonable supply of proper food, along with a flask of brandy. Into his wallet went a moderate sum of proper coins, silver and gold, and also a forged letter of credit on an Empire City bank. They hoped he would not need much money, and plans did not call for him to get within a hundred miles of the Holy City. But just in case.

Chan Amling was issued a somewhat worn and soiled grey friar's habit, and very little else, in keeping with his mendicant role. He did half-seriously request permission to take along a pair of dice, arguing that he would not be the first friar in history to go so armed. But Time ops soon established that such equipment was hardly standard issue for the religious, even in Vincento's time, and turned down the request.

Both Derron and Chan had hung round their necks abominably carved wooden wedge-symbols. The images differed in detail of design, but each was big enough to conceal the bulk of a miniaturized communicator, and too ugly and cheap-looking for anyone to want to steal. If any of Vincento's contemporaries were moved to wonder audibly why Derron wore such a thing, he was to say it was a present from his wife.

From an arsenal assembled in Stage Three, Odegard and Amling were both issued sturdy travellers' staffs. These again were dissimilar in outer detail but were both more effective weapons by far than they appeared to be. All of the agents were armed, with staffs or other innocent-appearing devices; they were all going to be dropped within half a minute of one another, present-time, though of course they were to arrive in different places and on different days.

Their processing for this mission had been too hurried and too much individualized for them to get to know one another very well. But during the last few minutes before the drop, as the masquerade-costumed group bade one another good luck and good berserker-hunting, there was joking camaraderie in Stage Three.

Derron felt it. It crossed his mind that now he had good friends among the living once more. The launching file formed on the order, and he took his place in it calmly, looking forward over short Chan Amling's grey-cowled head.

Amling turned his head slightly. "Five will get you ten," he offered, whispering, "that I land up to my crotch in mud someplace. Out of sight of the bloody road, at least."

"No bet," said Derron automatically, as the count began. The line moved briskly forward, one figure after another in front of him abruptly vanishing from his sight. Amling made some last remark that Derron could not catch, and then Amling too was gone.

It was Derron's turn. He swung a booted foot in a long stride out over the mercurial launching circle, and brought it down.

He was standing in darkness, and around him was the unmistakable, never-to-be-forgotten feeling of open air. Except for a mere whisper of breeze and a drizzle of rain, he was immersed in an echoless silence, a great loneliness in which his materialization must have passed unnoticed. Good.

"Reverend Brother?" he enquired of the darkness in a low voice, speaking of course in Vincento's language. There was no answer; Amling might well have come down in some mudhole out of sight of the road. He had a knack for achieving what he was willing to bet on.

As Derron's eyes grew more accustomed to the gloom he made out that the hard surface under his own boots did indeed seem to be that of the old Empire highway which passed through Oibbog. Operations had put at least half of the team spatially on the bull's-eye, then. Whether they had done as well temporally remained to be seen, though rain and darkness were reassuring signs.

Subvocalizing, Derron tried to reach Operations for a routine check-in, but the communicator seemed utterly dead. Some kind of paradox-loop would be blocking contact. Such things cropped up now and then; there was nothing to do but hope that the condition would not last long.

He waited the agreed-upon few minutes for Amling, meanwhile opening his staff at one end and consulting the compass thus revealed, to make sure of the direction he was facing on the road. Then, after calling once more for his Reverend Brother without result, he began to walk, boots clopping solidly on the pavement. Lightning flashed distantly, at irregular intervals. He drank deep breaths of the washed air.

He had not gone far before the transducer behind his ear gave him a sudden twinge. ". . . Odegard, can you read me yet? Colonel Odegard . . ." The male voice had a weary, bored tone.

"This is Colonel Odegard, I read you."

"Colonel!" Sudden excitement. Off mike: "We've got contact, sir!" Back on: "Colonel, it's plus two days and three hours here since you were dropped. Time scale has been slipping."

"Understand." Derron kept his speech subvocal. "I'm about plus five minutes since dropping. Still on the road in the rain, at night. No contact with Amling yet."

"Odegard, you're blurring on the screens." It was Time Ops' voice speaking now. "But it looks like you're farther from the cathedral than we intended, just about two miles. You may be outside the safety zone, so get in closer to Vincento as fast as possible." By safety zone, Time Ops of course meant the zone of protection against any direct violence from the berserker, a zone created by the intense concentration of sentry observation round Vincento's lifeline. "We've just pulled the team ahead of you out. They report all's well with Vincento. You say you haven't seen Amling yet."

"Right." Derron stepped up his pace a trifle, though he was having to tap along with his staff to be sure of not floundering off the pavement into the mud.

"We haven't found him either. Can't see his line in this blurring on the screens. It may be just the time-slippage and a paradox-loop."

Lightning flared straight ahead of Derron, obligingly showing him that his road ran straight for some distance in that direction, and that the cathedral spire was there, though farther off than it should have been. He supposed it was just about two miles away.

He reported this to Operations, meanwhile puzzling about something else, much nearer, that the lightning had also shown him—a dully gleaming object lying in the centre of the road, atop a line or thin trench that seemed to have been scratched or dug across the way.

". . . I'm just coming up to it now. Looks like . . ."

It was soft to the prodding tip of his staff. He waited for the lightning, which came again in a few seconds.

"Never mind trying to contact Amling any more." The body was quite naked; it might have been here a day or an hour. Derron stood over it describing the situation as best he could. Human robbers might have stolen a staff and even a cheap pectoral wedge, but would they have taken a friar's habit. . . ?

He bent to touch the deep scratch mark that cut across the road beneath the body. No medieval tool had made that ruler-straight slice through stone; quite likely it had been carved by the same cybernetic limb that had removed the back of Amling's head.

"Ops, I think it's marked the boundary of the safety zone for us. To let us know that it knows about it."

"Yes, yes, you may be right about that, Odegard, but never mind it now. You just move in close to Vincento quickly, protect yourself."

He was moving that way already, walking backward and holding his staff like a rifle while all his senses probed as best they could the rainy night through which he had just passed. Not that all his alertness would do him any good, if the enemy was out there and able to strike.

But Derron lived. After a hundred paces he turned and walked normally ahead, once more making good time. The berserker had killed casually, in passing, leaving its mark like some defiant human outlaw. And then it had gone on, to press its real business here.

By the time Derron had reached the place where the road bent sharply to the left toward the washed-out bridge, the lightning had gone on over the horizon; he felt rather than saw the bulk of the hill and its cathedral ahead of him and above. But nearer, close by the side of the road, he could make out the monastry's high wall, the tumbled stones of what had been an arched gateway, and the remnants of a broken gate. And when he stood just before the gateway he could distinguish, just inside, a coach that he knew must be Vincento's, standing deserted in a puddle. From the shelter of a cloister came the gentle mumbling and grunting of loadbeasts. Derron paused only a moment before plodding on through the gate and across a soggy garth toward what looked like the main entrance of the main building, which was a sprawling one-storey structure.

He made no effort to be quiet, and the dark doorway before him promptly emitted a challenge. "Who's there? Stand and give your name!"

The dialect was one of those Derron had expected to run into. He stopped in his tracks, and as the beam of a lantern flicked out at him, answered: "I am Valzay of Mosnar, mathematicus and scholar. From the coach and animals I see here, I judge that you within are honest men. And I have need of shelter."

"Step for'ard then," said the wary male voice that had challenged him. A door creaked, and behind the door the lantern retreated.

Derron advanced slowly, displaying hands empty save for an innocent staff. When he had gotten in out of the rain the door was shut behind him and the lantern brightened. He found himself in what must have been the common room of the monastery. Facing him stood a pair of soldiers, one armed with a crude pistol and the other with a short sword; judging by their patchwork uniforms they were members of one of the mercenary companies that were now multiplying in this war-torn land.

When they could see his gentleman's clothes more plainly, the soldiers' manner became more or less respectful. "Well, sir, how d'you come to be a-wanderin' afoot and alone?"

He scowled and swore, wringing water from his cloak. He related how his skittish loadbeast, scared by lightning, had run off with his light sulky. A plague was too good for that animal! If he could catch it in the morning, he'd have some of its hide off in narrow strips, they could bet on that! With whip-cracking vehemence he shook water from his broad-brimmed hat.

Derron had an effortless feel and skill for acting when there was a need for it, and these lines had been well rehearsed. The soldiers chuckled, relaxed most of their vigilance, and became willing to chat. There was, they said, plenty of room for another boarder here, because the proprietary monks had all cleared out long ago. The place was no tavern with girls and ale, worse luck, and even firewood was in short supply, but the roof did keep the rain off. Yes, they were from a mercenary company, one which was now in the pay of the Holy Temple. Their captain, with the bulk of his men, was now in Oibbog across the river.

"And if the cap'n can't do no more'n wave to us for the next couple days, why that's all right with us, hey what?"

For all the jocularity, they still maintained a minimal professional suspicion of Derron—he might conceivably be a scout for some well-organized band of brigands—and so they did not tell him how many soldiers had been caught on this side of the torrent when the bridge they had been guarding collapsed. He did not ask, of course, but he gathered there were not many.

Answering a question he did ask, one of the soldiers said: "Naw, no one but the old gentleman as owns the coach, and his servant an' his driver. And a pair o' friars. Plenty empty cells, sir, so take your pick. One's about as damp as the next."

Derron murmured his thanks, and then with some brief assistance from the lantern groped his way down a vaulted passage lined with doorless cells, and into one of these which was pointed out to him as unoccupied. Built against the cell's rear wall was a wooden bunk frame that had not yet been ripped out for firewood. On this Derron sat down to pull off his squelching boots, while the lantern's light receded once more down the passage and vanished.

His boots off and tipped to drain, Derron stretched out on the wooden frame, knapsack under his head, dry garment from knapsack over him for cover, his staff within easy reach. He did not yet have the feeling of having achieved his goal and returning to Oibbog. Amling's death seemed a bit unreal. Neither was it quite graspable that Vincent Vincento in the living flesh was somewhere within a few metres of him, that one of the founding fathers of the Modern world might even be the author of the snore that now drifted faintly down the passage.

Lying on his wooden bed, Derron reported briefly to Operations, bringing them up to the minute on his progress so far; then, genuinely tired, he found himself drifting toward sleep. The sound of rain was lulling, and there was nothing he could do about getting a look at Vincento until the morning. Even as his consciousness dulled it struck him as mildly odd that his thoughts were not occupied with his mission for Operations, nor with his private mission of return. Not with the staggering fact of time-travel, nor the loss of Amling, nor the menace of the berserker. Simply with the fading sound of diminishing rain, and the freshness of the infinite clean atmosphere around him. It was the theme of resurrection....

He was jarred out of the beginning of sleep when Operations put a throbbing behind his right ear. He came wide awake at once, with only a mild start, and tucked his carven wedge-symbol closer under his chin.

"Odegard, we're starting to read through some of this blurring on the screens. We can count fourteen lifelines in or near that monastery-temple complex. One of them of course is your own. Another is Vincento's. Another one seems to be an unborn child's line, you know how they show on a screen in dots and dashes."

Derron shifted his position slightly on the creaking wooden rack; he felt oddly comfortable and snug, hearing the last dripping of the rain outside. He mused subvocally: "Let's see. Me, Vincento, his two servants, and the two soldiers I've seen. That makes six. And they said there were two friars. Eight, which would leave six more unaccounted for. Probably four more soldiers, and a camp-follower who's picked up a little dotted line she won't want to carry. Wait a minute, though, that one soldier did say something about there being no girls here. Anyway, I suppose your idea is that one of the apparent people I find here will have no lifeline showing on your screens —meaning he or she is really our hypothetical berserker-android."

"That's our idea, yes."

"Tomorrow I can count noses and . . . wait."

In the darkness of the entrance to Derron's cell, a shape of lesser blackness became discrete with movement. The figure of a hooded friar, utterly faceless in the gloom, came a half-step into the cell before halting abruptly.

Derron froze, recalling the hooded robe missing from Amling's corpse. His hand moved to his staff, to grip it tightly. But he would not dare to use his weaponry, without being very sure of his target. Even then, at this close range, the staff before he could aim it would be torn from his hands and broken. . . .

Only an instant had passed since the hooded figure had entered. Now it muttered a few indistinguishable words, that might have been an apology for entering the wrong cell. And in another moment it had withdrawn into the blackness, as noiselessly as it had come.

Derron remained half-risen on one elbow, still gripping his useless weapon. He told Operations what had just happened.

"It won't dare kill you there, remember. Be very sure before you fire."

"Understand." Slowly he stretched out again. But all comfort had gone with the last of the rain, and resurrection was a lie.

When Vincento was awakened by a touch, and found himself in darkness, bedded amid damp straw, with bare stone walls close about him, he knew a moment of sinking terror. The worst had already happened and he lay in the Defenders' dungeon. The terror was deepened when he saw the faceless monk-hooded figure bending over him. He could see it by the moonlight which now filtered through the tiny window— evidently the rain was over——

The rain . . . of course, he was still on his way to the Holy City, his trial was still to come! The intensity of his relief was such that Vincento accepted almost with courtesy his being awakened. "What do you want?" he muttered, sitting up on his shelf of a bed and pulling his travelling-rug closer about his shoulders. His manservant Will slept on, a huddled mound on the dark floor.

The visitor's hooded face could not be seen. The visitor's voice was a sepulchral whisper: "Messire Vincento, you are to come alone to the cathedral tomorrow morning. At the cross-ways of nave and transepts you will receive good news, from your friends in high places."

He tried to digest this. Could it be that Nabur or perhaps Belam wanted to send him some secret reassurance of leniency? That was possible. More likely, this was some Defenders' trickery. A man summoned to trial was not supposed to discuss the matter with anyone.

"It will be good news, Messire Vincento. Come alone, and be willing to wait if you are not met at once. The crossways of nave and transepts. And do not seek to learn my name or face."

Vincento maintained his silence, determined to commit himself to nothing. And his visitor, satisfied that the message had been delivered, melted away into the night.

When Vincento awakened the next time, it was from a pleasant dream. He had been back in his own villa, on the estate which had been provided for him by the Senate of his city, safe in his own bed with his mistress's warm body solid and comforting beside him. In reality the woman had been gone for some time—women no longer meant very much—but the estate was still there. If only they would let him return to it in peace!

This time he had been aroused by a touch of a different sort—the touch on his face of a shaft of morning sunlight, which came striking into his cell from the high thin window of the cell across the corridor. As he lay recalling with curiosity his strange midnight visitor, making sure in his own mind that *that* had been no dream, the sun-shaft was already moving slowly away from his face. And instantly that motion made it a golden pendulum of subtle torture, driving all other thoughts from his mind.

The pendulum he really faced was that of choice. His mind could swing one way, *tick*, and meet in foresight the shame of swallowed truth and swallowed pride, all the humiliation of an enforced recanting. And if he swung his thoughts the other way, *tock*, there they confronted the breaking agony of the boot or the rack, or the slower destruction in a buried cell.

It was not a dozen years since the Defenders had burned Onadroig alive in the Great Square of the Holy City. Of course Onadroig had been no scientist, but rather a poet and a philosopher. The consensus these days among scholars was that he must have also been a madman, an utter fanatic who had walked into a fire rather than give over his theories. And what theories had possessed him! He had believed that the Holy One had been no more than a magician; that the chief of devils would one day be saved; that there were infinite worlds in space, that the very stars were peopled.

Neither in the Scriptures nor in nature could the least justification for any of these absurd ideas be found—so Belam and the other Defenders had argued, indefatigably but fruitlessly trying to change Onadroig's mind during the seven years' imprisonment that had preceded his burning as an incorrigible heretic.

To Vincento himself, the crude physical torture was a remote threat only. He or any other reputable scholar would have to show very deliberate and prolonged stubbornness before the Defenders would employ any such methods against him. But the threat would be in the background, all the same. At his trial he would be formally threatened with torture, perhaps even shown the instruments. All ritual, no more. But it was not impossible that it should become more. *They* would say, with genuine unhappiness, that a defendant who absolutely refused to yield to all milder methods of persuasion forced them to take harsh measures, for the good of his immortal soul and the protection of the Faith.

So—his pendulum of choice was not real. He had no real choice but to recant. Let the sun move any way they wanted it to. Let it go whirling round the globe in an insane yearly spiral, to please the arrogant short-sighted fools who thought they had already read all the secrets of the universe, in a few dusty pages of the Holy Writings.

Lying on his back, Vincento raised a hand veined with ropey vessels against the slow-swivelling torture-blade of the sun. But the sun would not be stopped in its motion by any man's hand. It mocked him all the more, making bright translucent wax out of the oldness of his fingers.

On the floor, Will stirred sluggishly in his rug-cocoon. Vincento barked him awake, and chased him out to rouse the coachman, Rudd, who slept beside the beasts—Rudd to look at the river's level, Will to make some tea and get a little food ready for breakfast. Vincento had had the foresight to provision his coach well.

Left alone, he began the slow humiliating process of getting his aging bones unlimbered and ready for what the day might bring. In recent years his health had been poor, and now each day began with a cautious testing of sensation. But he was not sick now, only old. And, yes, he was afraid.

By the time Will came to inform him that a fire and hot tea were ready in the monastery's common room, Vincento was ready to step forth. Somewhat to his surprise, he discovered when he entered the common room that another wayfarer had arrived during the night, a youngster who introduced himself as Valzay of the distant land of Mosnar.

Valzay, as he put it himself, made a modest claim to scholarship. Hearing this, Vincento studied him more carefully. But, for a wonder, the youngster was decently respectful, seeming to regard Vincento with genuine if restrained awe, and murmuring that even in his distant homeland Vincento's discoveries were known and praised.

Vincento acknowledged all this with pleasant nods, meanwhile sipping his breakfast tea and wondering if this youth was the bearer of the good news he was supposed to hear this morning from someone in the cathedral. *Might* it after all be a word of hope from Nabur? He scowled. No, he would not let himself hope, like a vassal, for another man's kindness, not even when the other was the Vicar of the Holy One himself.

He straightened his back. Anyway, he was not going to rush up the hill to the temple at once.

Rudd came to report that the river was no longer rising, but was still too high and dangerous for anyone to think of trying to ford it here. In one more day it would probably be safe.

So Vincento took his time at finishing his tea and consuming a little food. He left word with Rudd to take some food to the two friars, and then strolled leisurely out into the sunshine to warm his bones. If he came late to his trial, there were plenty of witnesses here to tell the reason. Let the Defenders inveigh against the river, if they liked. No doubt the torrent would defer to their superior knowledge of the Holy Writings, and dry up. No doubt all of nature would do their bidding; likely the ruined bridge here would rebuild itself if they came to threaten the stones with torture.

But no, away with such thoughts, he must begin to practise his humility. He called to Will to fetch him his writing materials from the coach, and then he went out through the broken gate to sit alone in the sun beside the road, with one tumbled block of stone for a bench and another for a table. He might as well put his time to use, and start writing his statement of recantation to present during the trial.

Of course the accused was not supposed to know why he had been summoned. Probably the Defenders' first question would be whether or not he had any idea what he had been charged with. No doubt such an opening sometimes brought unsuspected crimes bursting to light from guilty lips, but in Vincento's case there could hardly be any doubt of the reason for his summons. It had been fifteen years since Belam's warning injunction, which Vincento himself had since managed to half-forget. Other scholars before and since had talked of the heliocentric hypothesis with impunity, and had used it in their published calculations. But when the Defenders' summons came, Vincento realized that he had bitterly antagonized men who were in high places and who never forgot anything.

The first paper he pulled from his portable escritoire was the old letter of injunction from Defender Belam. Involuntarily Vincento's eye went at once to the words: ". . . no proof of our globe's motion exists, as I believe, since none has been shown to me."

No proof. Vincento wiped at his forehead with a tremulous hand. Now, with mortal fear to enforce bleak clarity of thought, he could see that the arguments he had conjured from tides and sunspots really proved nothing at all about the motions of sun and planets. The truth about those motions had become apparent to him before he had ever thought of need for proving it. He had looked long through telescopes, and he had thought long and deeply about what he saw. With eyes and mind he had weighed the sun, he had grasped at stars and planets and comets, and truth had come through some inward door, like a revelation.

His enemies who cried him down were of course far lesser men than he. They were stupid and blind in their refusal, or their inability, to see what he showed them as the truth. And yet he knew that those who were to sit as his judges were shrewd enough logicians when they set themselves to think within their formal rules. If only there were some firm proof, simple and incontrovertible, that he might set before them . . . oh, what would he not give for that! His mind ached, his fists clenched, his very guts contracted at the thought. If he had one solid simple proof he would risk all, he would dare anything, to confront and confound his enemies with it, to rub their long arrogant noses in the truth!

But since in fact he had nothing to support this mood of glorious defiance, it soon passed. The truth was, he was old and afraid, and he was going to recant.

Slowly he got out pen and ink and blank paper, and slowly he began his first draft. From time to time he paused, sitting with closed eyes in the sun, trying not to think.

Derron counted seven soldiers round the breakfast fire, and he found each of them overjoyed to accept a swallow of brandy from his travelling flask, and willing enough to talk. No, there was no one he had not seen in the monastery or the cathedral, or anywhere nearer than the town across the river. Not that they knew of, and they would know.

When he was alone in the privy a few minutes later, Derron did some subvocal mumbling. "Operations?"

"Time Ops here."

Maybe the Commander never had to sleep, but Derron himself was sufficiently tired and strained to dispense with military courtesy. "Count the lifelines here again. I make it just thirteen of us. If you can make it twelve, then one of my smiling companions has clockwork for guts. But if you come out with *fourteen* again, then either there's some bandit or deserter lurking in a corner I haven't seen, or you're misreading your screens. I think that dotted line at least is a mistake in interpretation; I consider it unlikely that any of us here is pregnant, since we're all men."

"We'll recheck right away. You know how tricky screen interpretation can be sometimes." Time Ops' tone was quietly apologetic, which was somehow more disturbing to Derron than a chewing-out would have been. It meant that his position here was now considered so vital that Operations would bend every effort to make things go more smoothly for him.

The soldiers, after finishing their morning meal and emptying Derron's brandy flask, had for the most part settled down to serious loafing. Rudd, Vincento's coachman, was leading his loadbeasts forth in search of grass. Following the animals through the gate, Derron located Vincento, sitting peacefully alone and apart with his writing materials. Well and good.

Remembering his imaginary loadbeast and sulky, Derron put on an exasperated expression and strolled along the road toward the bridge-stump, scanning the fields in all directions as if in search of his missing property.

At the bridge-stump were the two friars, grey cowls thrown back from their unremarkable heads. Judging by their gestures and a word or two which floated Derron's way, they were talking of ways in which the bridge might sometime be rebuilt. Derron knew that within a year or two there would indeed be new arches of stone spanning the river here. And those arches would still be standing solidly more than three hundred years later, when a young post-graduate history student would come striding over them on a hiking tour, the girl he loved striding just as eagerly beside him. Both of them would be enthusiastic about seeing for the first time the ancient town and the famed cathedral of Oibbog . . . the river would look much different then, gentler of course, and there would be more trees along its banks. While the stones of the ancient Empire road would still look much the same . . .

"May the Holy One give you a good day, esteemed sir!" It

was the stouter of the two friars whose voice broke in upon the start of reverie.

The interruption was welcome. "Good day to you also, reverend brothers. Does the river still rise?"

The thinner friar had a loving face. In hands all bone and tendon he was weighing a small chunk of masonry, as if he meant to start this minute to rebuild the bridge. "The river falls now, sir. How does the course of your life go, up or down?"

The falsehood about beast and buggy seemed dreary and unnecessary. "That can hardly be an easy question for any man to answer."

Derron was spared any further probing for the moment, as both friars were distracted. Seven or eight of the local peasantry had materialized out of mud and distance and were plodding their barefoot way along the drying bank of the torrent toward the bridge-stump. One man walking in front of the others proudly swung a string of large and silvery fish, fresh enough to be still twitching and twisting.

A few paces away from the edge of the pavement the peasants halted. Together they bowed rather perfunctorily in Derron's direction; he was not dressed finely enough to overawe anyone, and he was obviously not the one the peasants had come to see.

The man who carried the fish began talking to the friars, in a low tone at first but raising his voice as the others began almost at once to interrupt him. In a few moments they were all squabbling over who had the right to speak first, and whose was the right of disposal of the fish. They had come to strike a bargain. Would the holy brothers accept the biggest and freshest of this fine catch ("From me! No, from *me*, Holy Brother, it was my fishline!") and in return say some potent prayers for the giver's crops?

Derron turned away from what promised to become a nasty quarrel among the peasants, to see that Vincento was still sitting alone. And it was then that the full sunlit view of the Cathedral of Oibbog caught him almost by surprise.

The narrowed tip of the central spire held its gilded symbolic wedge two hundred and sixty feet above the flattened hilltop. The stones of tower and wall, of arch and flying buttress, were rich clear grey, almost shining in the morning light.

Inside, he knew, the stained glass windows along the eastern wall would be like living flame. If fragile glass and spire had risen from the dust, then surely she too must be alive, not only alive but somewhere near where he might reach her. At the moment the resurrected reality before him held more conviction than any rein of logic. At any second now her voice might call him, he might be able to reach out and touch . . .

There was a splash nearby. The stout friar was wearing a caricature-expression of anger, disappointment, and surprise, while the thinner one stood with a hand stretched out over the water. A big fish now jumped and splashed again; one of the slippery catch had evidently escaped.

. . . touch her warm and living skin. Now even a detail that he had somehow forgotten, the way her hair moved sometimes in the wind, came back to him with the visual clarity of something seen only a minute ago.

Derron's feet took him away from the bridge-stump, back along the road. He noted dutifully with half his mind that Vincento still sat alone in the sun. But Derron did not go back to the monastery. The hill raised the mighty cathedral before him, and his feet began a steady climb.

Brother Jovann kept looking sadly at the peasants, even as he seemed to address his words to the splasher in the water. "Brother Fish, I have set you at liberty not because we do not need food, but so you may be able to praise God, who sends all blessings—the fish to the angler, or freedom to the fish." Sorrowfully Jovann shook his head at the peasants. "We men so often forget to give thanks when they are due, so often we spend our energy instead in trying to get ahead of one another!"

The fish splashed, and leaped, and splashed again. As if the pain of the hook, or the time spent gilling air—or something else—had driven it quite mad.

Jovann looked down with new distress upon this watery uproar. "Be still now, Brother Fish! Enough! Live in the water, not the painful air. Give praise and thanks as a fish may naturally do!"

The splashing stopped. The last ripples and foam of it were swept away downstream.

Silence hung in the air. Every peasant's hands were raised in the wedge-sign, and they darted their eyes at one another as if they would have liked to take to their heels in flight, but did not dare. Brother Saile was gaping as blankly as any of the fish, while he swung his eyes from Jovann to the river and back again.

Jovann beckoned Saile away, and said to him: "I am going apart for an hour, to pray to the Holy One to cleanse me of anger and pride. And also for these poor men's crops. Do you likewise." And Saile was left still gaping as Jovann walked slowly away alone, on up the road toward the monastery's gate.

As Derron climbed the steps that switchbacked up the face of the cathedral hill, the irrational sense of his love's presence faded, leaving him with only the bitter certainty of her permanent loss. It crossed his mind that at this moment in time her genes were scattered in the chromosomes of some two thousand ancestors. That was as close as he could come to her today, and the closest he would ever be able to come. He knew that a solid palisade of paradox-loops would forever bar him from revisiting the days of her life, what he thought of as the time of his own youth.

The truth was that he had never forgiven her for dying, for being helplessly killed with all the other millions, for her crime of emptying his world. Maybe forgiving her was what he had come back to Oibbog to try to do. So, he told himself, do it. Do whatever is necessary to end it now, today. Get it all over with somehow, out of your system once and for all, so you can be some good to yourself and to someone else again.

By now the roof of the monastery had fallen below the level of his climbing feet. When he looked back he saw the valley spreading out, flood-ravaged now and wilder in its beauty than he remembered it, but still essentially the same. At a turn on the stairs he passed a sapling, and with a pang of realization knew that in three hundred years this slender stem would be a gnarled and mighty trunk, with heavy branches to shade out the summer sun. And beside it he would stand with her, looking out over the valley, the two of them picking out a hill for themselves—that hill there, oh God, though no trees were on it now!—where one day they intended to build their home and raise the pair of kids they meant to have.

He kept right on climbing, because he felt that if he stopped here now he might never go on, and going on was necessary. Now at last his eyes rose above the level of the paved space before the main entrance of the cathedral. His memory recognized the very pattern of the paving stones here, where her feet and his would one day stand. If he stood here now, looking straight ahead at remembered hedges and statues, his vision bounded by the grey stone of the cathedral's front—why, for all that he could see or hear, holiday and youth and love might still be true, war and grief no more than bad dreams passing.

The twigs of the hedges were green again, with rain and late spring sunshine. But her voice was not to be heard here, nor would he ever again feel her touch, though he were to stand here till he fell. And for a moment he thought he might be going to fall, or to kneel and pray, or to cry aloud, because the knowledge of her passing from him was almost too much—but then, at long long last, that knowledge could be accepted.

The process of acceptance was not over in an instant, but once it had fairly begun he knew he was not going to collapse. His eyes were none too clear, but he was not going to weep. He was just going to stand here and go on living.

No, he was not finished yet. To complete the process of acceptance and release he had still to go into the building, where he had spent a morning helping her photograph stained glass. He remembered wishing aloud at that time that the supposed author of the universe would come out of hiding and make an appearance in this, supposedly his temple; because the young historian had a few sharp questions that he wanted to ask. Questions having to do with the unnecessary amount of injustice in the world.

The main door was just as solidly hung as Derron remembered it. He wondered briefly if a wooden door in steady use might last three hundred years. No matter. He tugged it open, and heard the booming reverberation of the broken closure come back with repetitions from the building's cavernous interior. Just then it crossed Derron's mind that his traveller's staff with all its weaponry was resting back in his monastery cell. But that was no matter; immediate violence from the berserker was not a danger.

He went in and paced down the centre of the nave, which

was only about thirty feet wide between the rows of columns which divided it from the side aisles, but enormous in its other dimensions—three hundred feet long, the keystones of its arches a hundred feet above the floor. There seemed room in here for god and berserker both to hide, with plenty of corners left to conceal some deserter or pregnant waif whose lifeline might be showing up to confuse Operations.

Along the eastern wall the stained-glass windows flamed. Centuries of candle smoke had not yet darkened the high arches. Most of the cathedral had been built during the last generation; in fact construction had not been quite completed when this latest war had resulted in the workmen being ordered or frightened off the job. Much scaffolding still surrounded columns and clung to walls, here and there festooned with the workmen's abandoned ropes and cables, which were as steady in the motionless air as if carved from stone themselves. A few abandoned tools were very slowly gathering dust where they had been set down.

Whether because of the combatants' reverence or superstitious fear, or only through chance, war had not trampled here. Even the stained glass was all intact, splintered only by the sun coming in to fire the mild gloom with richness. The wide steps which led to side chapels, and most of the paving of the nave, were no more than a century old, still flat and practically unworn; three centuries and more of random footsteps would be required to shape them into standard distribution curves.

As Derron approached the centre of the building, where nave and transepts intersected, a movement caught the corner of his eye. One of the friars, hood worn over his head here in God's house, was approaching him down a side aisle.

Derron stopped, nodding politely. "Reverend Brother." And then it struck him as odd, that one of the men he had left down at the bridge should have hurried here ahead of him. Peering closely, he saw that the face beneath the cowl was not quite a face. And the hands reaching to grab him as the figure shot forward were dummy flesh, split open now to show the steel claws.

The leaner of the friars had come dragging along, head bowed, up the road from the bridge-stump. He passed the monastery's gateway, and Vincento was just thinking with some relief that the man was going right on by him, when at the last moment the friar appeared to become aware of Vincento, and after a little startled pause changed course and came toward him.

He stopped a couple of paces away, smiling now, a gentle and bedraggled figure. "God will reward you, Vincent, for providing my companion and me with food."

"God knows I have some need of His favour, brother," Vincento answered shortly. He supposed the mendicant had learned his given name from Rudd or Will. Curiously he did not feel offended by the familiar form of address; the dusty beggar before him seemed, like an infant, beneath any question of status.

But Vincento remained wary. It was just possible that this friar was one of the Defenders' agents.

The friar was looking at the papers before Vincento as he might have regarded some friend's unbandaged wound. "Vincent, why do you waste your mind and soul in all these struggles and disputes? Their outcome does not matter, really. But one thing matters, and that is the love of God."

The mad innocent sincerity of this all but wiped away Vincento's suspicions, and could provoke him to nothing stronger than a smile. "It seems you have taken the trouble to learn something of my affairs. But, Reverend Brother, what do you really understand of my disputes and why I have them?"

The friar drew back, with a little quiver of distaste. "I do not understand them. I do not wish to, it is not my way."

"Then, brother, pardon me, but it seems to me you should not lecture on what you do not understand, nor stand here disputing with me as to why I have disputes."

The friar accepted the rebuke so meekly that Vincento felt a momentary pang of something like regret for having spoken it. And with that the dispute between them, if they could really call it that, was over, Vincento having scored his point with the ease of an armoured knight knocking down a child.

The friar did not turn away before he had raised his hands in blessing and murmured a few words that were not addressed to Vincento. Then he departed at once, walking slowly on along the road—once hesitating as if on the point of turning back, then going on. It crossed Vincento's mind that he had once again won an argument and perhaps lost something else—though what it was one lost on these occasions he could not exactly say. He almost called after the man, feeling an impulse to try to reach across the gap between them. But he did not call. Really, he thought, we have nothing to say to each other.

Anyway, now that he had been distracted from the humiliating task of writing his recantation, he did not want to take it up again. And so Vincento summoned Will, gave him the escritoire and papers to take in charge, and then turned his own steps restlessly upward in the fine sunlight.

Thinking it over now, he decided that the meeting supposedly arranged in the cathedral was most probably some snare of the Defenders—or more likely, of some of Vincento's enemies, religious or laymen, who would be eager to trick him into some compromising utterance or behaviour on the eve of his trial. Very well, let them try. He would see through the scheme, whatever it was, before they had gotten very far with it. He might be able to turn the tables on them completely. Vincento might fear men who overmatched him in power, but he knew full well that none could do so in intelligence.

He was patient with his old legs, resting them for a single breath after every two or three steps, and so they served him well enough on the climb. After a longer pause for rest at the top of the stairs, he entered at the cathedral's main door, and tugged it firmly closed behind him. He devoutly hoped that no one was going to meet him simply to offer sympathy. A sympathizer was at best a secret gloater, having always at least some implied claim to be the equal—more likely the superior!—of the one he supposedly was trying to console. Pah!

Vincento strolled through the nave, a stone-sealed space too vast to give the least sense of confinement. To his right and left the vault-supporting columns towered in their parallel rows. Distance diminished the apparent space between each column and the next, until at fifty paces ahead of him each row became opaque as a wall. No matter where a man stood inside this unpartitioned space, half of it would always be blocked from his view—more than half, if one counted the areas of the transept-arms and the chapels.

When he reached the appointed meeting place, the crossways of nave and transepts, Vincento could look directly up nearly two hundred feet, into the shadowed interior of the temple's mighty central spire. There were workmen's platforms even there, reached by ladders mounting from the clerestory level, which in turn must be accessible by some stair coiling up within the wall from the level of the floor Vincento stood upon.

In this temple, built in the grand old style, there were no chandeliers, and no breezes to swing them if they had existed. If in Vincento's youth this had been his parish house of worship, he would have had to begin to work out the laws of pendulums somewhere else, and not during a drowsy Sabbath sermon.

A single cable of great length descended thinly from the uttermost dark interior of the spire. Vincento's eye followed this cable down, to discover that there was a pendulum here after all, at least in potential. For bob, there hung on the end of the long cable a ball of metal that would be as heavy as a man. This weight was pulled to one side, held by the merest loop of cord to one of the four thick columns that stood at corners of the nave-transept intersection.

Looking up and down, up and down again, tended to make an old man dizzy. Vincento rubbed his neck. But there was an offence to logic here that was beyond his power to ignore. What use could the builders have had for such a patriarch of pendulums?

It *could*, he supposed, be something they swung when hard stone and mortar had to be demolished—that was hardly a satisfactory explanation. And if it was only a plumb-line, why so weighty? A few ounces of lead would serve that purpose just as well.

Whatever they had intended or used it for, it *was* a pendulum. The restraining tether of cord, with its single knot, looked insubstantial. Vincento thrummed the taut little cord with his finger, and the long long cable gently whipped and swayed. The massive weight made little bobbing motions, dipping like a ship at anchor.

The oscillations quickly died away, the stillness of the cathedral soon regained ascendancy. Once more cord and cable and bob were as steady as the stone columns in the still grey air. The pendulum-ship was drydocked.

Set sail, then! On impulse Vincento tugged once at the end

of the restraining cord. And with startling ease the knot dissolved.

Starting from rest, the weight for a moment seemed reluctant to move at all. And even after it had undeniably begun its first swing, still it moved so slowly that Vincento's eye went involuntarily racing once more up into the shadows of the spire, to see how it was possible that a mere length of cord should so delay things.

A man might have counted four without haste before the weight for the first time reached the centre, the low-point, of its swing. Almost touching the floor, it passed that centre in a smooth fast rush and immediately began to slow again, so that it needed four more counts to climb the gentle gradient of the far half of its arc. Then the weight paused for an unmeasurable instant, not quite touching the column at the opposite corner of the crossways, before it crept into its returning motion.

Majestically the bob went back and forth, holding its cable taut, describing a perfect arc-segment about ten yards in length. Vincento's eye could find no diminution in the amplitude of the first half-dozen swings. He supposed that a weight so heavy and so freely suspended as this might continue to oscillate for many hours or even for days.

Wait, though. Here was something. Vincento squinted at the pendulum through a swing. Then, leaning against the column it had been tethered to, and holding his head motionless, he watched the pendulum's swing end-on for another half-dozen cycles.

What was it he had come in here for? Oh yes, someone was perhaps going to meet him.

But this pendulum. He frowned at it, shook his head and watched some more. Then he started to look around him. He was going to have to make sure of something he thought he saw.

Some workmen's sawhorses were standing not far away. He dragged a pair of these to where he wanted them, so that the plank he now took up and set across them lay beneath the end of the pendulum's arc, and perpendicular to that arc's direction. On the bottom of the swinging weight he had noticed a projection like a small spike—whatever it had been meant for, it would serve Vincento's present purpose well. He laid a second plank atop the first, and slightly readjusted the position of his whole structure, in careful increments. Now on each swing the spike passed within an inch of the topmost board.

He could make marks upon the board... but no, he could do better. Somewhere in here he had seen sand. Yes, piled in a mixing-trough, there by the entrance to the first side-chapel. The sand was satisfactorily damp from the long spell of wet weather; he brought handfuls of it and dumped them on his upper board. Along several feet of the board's length he patted and built the sand into a tiny wall, an inch or two high and just thick enough to stand. Then, in an interval between swings, he slid that upper board just slightly forward, taking his sandwall into the edge of the pendulum's arc.

A neatly designed experiment, he thought with satisfaction. On its first return the moving spike notched his little sand-fence delicately, tumbling a tiny clot of grains down the minute slope. Then the weight pulled its taut cable away again, taking another slow nibble of eternity.

Vincento held his eyes from blinking as he watched the pendulum's return. Holding his breath too, he could now hear for the first time the faint ghostly hissing of the swing.

The spike coming back to the wall of sand made a new notch, though one contiguous to the first. Then the weight once more departed, in a movement huge and regular enough to be the cathedral's stately pulse.

And sixteen seconds later the third notch was new again, by the same margin and in the same direction as the second. In three vibrations the plane of the pendulum had shifted its extremity sideways by half a finger-width. His eyes had not deceived him earlier; that plane was slowly and regularly creeping clockwise.

Might this effect be due to some slow untwisting of the cable? Then it should soon reverse itself, Vincento thought, or at least vary in amplitude. Again he stared up into the high shadows, oblivious of his aching neck.

If he could, he would someday, somewhere, hang another pendulum like this one and study it at leisure. Yes, if he could. Even supposing that his health held out, and that he was spared prison, it would be difficult. Enclosed towers of this height were anything but common. In another big temple, or at some university perhaps—but he had no intention of stooping to collaboration.

. . . Suppose now that the puzzling sideways progression was *not* due to the cable's unwinding. He thought he could feel that it was not, in somewhat the same way as, after study, he had come to feel certain of the stability of the sun. This clockwise creeping had something too elemental about it for him to be able to credit a trivial cause.

Already the width of two fingers had been nibbled from the top of his little parapet of sand.

He wondered how the cable was fastened at the top. Younger legs than his would be required to find that out, and Vincento departed to obtain them. Several times in his passage down the nave he turned, frowning back at the ceaseless pendulum as he might have stared at an unexpected star.

Of it all, Derron had seen only an upper segment of the moving cable. He saw even that much with only one eye, for his face was being held with steady force against the rough planking of the high platform to which he had been carried, helpless as a kicking infant in the grip of the berserker. Inhumanly motionless, it crouched over him now, one chill hand gripping his neck and holding part of his coat gaglike in his mouth, the other hand twisting one of his arms just to the point of pain.

Obviously the machine had no intention of killing or crippling him, not here. Still, his captivity seemed less like a period of time than a segment of eternity, measured out by the meaningless regularity of the swinging cable. Having him prisoner, the berserker was content to wait, which meant he had already failed. He had not had time even to communicate his situation to Operations; the berserker had at once known his pectoral wedge for what it was; it had ripped the wooden carving from his neck and cracked it like a thin-shelled nut, squeezing the meat of metal and components into trash between its fingers.

Perhaps it thought that he could see nothing, from the position in which it held him. That was almost true. Only from the tail of one eye he could just descry that metronomic cable, its arc narrow at this height, but its slowness speaking of its enormous length.

At last the cathedral door far below boomed shut for the second time since he had been captured. And only then did eternity begin to come to an end; the berserker let him go.

Slowly and painfully he raised his half-numbed body from the wood. Rubbing the cheek that had been ground against the platform and the arm that had been twisted, he turned to face his enemy. Under the monk's cowl he saw a pattern of seamed metal that looked as if it might be able to open and slide and reshape itself. He knew that he was facing what was probably the most complex and compact machine that the berserkers had ever built. Inside that steel skull, could there be plastic skin that could evert to become the convincing mask of a human face? There was no way to tell that much, let alone guess what identity it might be able to wear.

"Colonel Odegard," it said, in a voice machine-tailored to neutrality.

Taken somewhat by surprise, he waited to hear more, while the thing facing him on the high platform squatted on its heels, arms hanging limp. The hands were as ambiguous as the face; they were not human now, but there was no saying what they might be able to become. The rest of the body was hidden under the shapeless robe, which had probably once been Amling's. "Colonel Odegard, do you fear the passage from life to not-life?"

He didn't know what he had expected to hear, but hardly that. "And if I do, what difference does it make?"

"Yes," said the berserker in its flat voice. "What is programmed goes on, regardless of any passage."

Before he could try to make any sense out of that, the machine jumped precisely forward and grabbed him again. He struggled again, which of course made no difference. It tore strips from his coat, ripping the tough cloth with precise and even sounds. With the strips it gagged him again, and tied him hand and foot—tightly, but not so tightly that he felt hopeless of ever working free. It was not going to blunder into being responsible for a death here in the safety zone.

After it had bound him, the machine paused for a moment, moving its cowled head like a listening man, searching the area with senses far beyond the human. And then it was gone down the ladder in utter silence, moving less like a man than like a giant cat or ape.

He could only strain desperately to get free, choking curses on his gag.

A second group of peasants, these from some village higher in the hills, had come along the road to the cathedral. It was Brother Saile they met first; when they learned that he was not the saint and miracle-worker of whom the whole countryside was talking a brief glow of hope died from their faces, leaving only bitter anxiety.

"Tell me, what is it you wish to see Brother Jovann about?" Saile inquired magisterially, clasping his hands with dignity across his belly.

They clamoured piteously, all at once, until he had to speak sharply to get them to talk one at a time and make sense. Then he heard that for several days past a great wolf had terrorized their little village. The monstrous beast had killed cattle, and even—they swore it!—uprooted crops. The peasants were all talking at once again, and Saile was not sure if they said a child had been devoured, or if a herdboy had fallen and broken his arm, trying to get away from the wolf. In any case the villagers were desperate. Men hardly dared to work their fields. They were isolated, and very poor, with no powerful patron to give them aid of any kind, save only the Holy One himself! And now the saintly Jovann, who must and would do *something*! They were utterly desperate!

Brother Saile nodded. In his manner there showed sympathy mixed with reluctance. "And you say your village is several miles distant? In the hills, yes. Well—we shall see. I will do my best for you. Come with me and I will put your case before good Brother Jovann."

With a puzzled Will now walking beside him, Vincento entered the cathedral once more, and made the best speed that he could down the nave. Down at the monastery Rudd had chosen this time to bother him with warnings and complaints about the scarcity of food for the beasts. And when he had disentangled himself from that, his old legs had rebelled against climbing the hill a second time, even with Will's help. Now as Vincento hurried, wheezing for breath, back to his still-swinging pendulum, more than an hour had passed since he had first set the bob in motion.

For a few seconds he only stared in thoughtful silence at

what had happened since his departure. The tiny battlement of sand had been demolished by continuous notches, up to the point where the pendulum's turning plane had left it behind altogether. That plane had by now inched clockwise through ten or twelve degrees of arc.

"Will, you've helped me in the workshop. Now this is another such case, where you must follow my orders precisely."

"Aye, master."

"First, keep in mind that you are not to stop the swinging of this cable here, or disturb it in any way. Understood?"

"Aye."

"Good. Now I want you to climb; there seem to be ladders and platforms enough for you to go up all the way. I want to discover how this swinging cable is mounted, what holds it at the top. Look at it until you can make me a sketch, you have a fair hand at drawing."

"Aye, I understand, sir." Will craned his neck unhappily. "It's a longish bit o' climbin', though."

"Yes, yes, a coin for you when you're down. Another when you've given me a good sketch. Take your time now, and use your eyes. And remember, do not disturb the cable's swing."

Derron had made only moderate progress toward getting the bonds loosened from his wrists when he heard clumsier feet than the berserker's climbing toward him. Then between the ladder's uprights Will's honest face came into view, to predictably register shock.

". . . bandit!" Derron spat, when his hands had been cut free and he could rid himself of the gag. "Must've been hiding in here somewhere . . . forced me up here and tied me up."

"Robbed ye, hey?" Will was awed. "Just one of 'em?"

"Yes, just one. Uh . . . I didn't have any valuables with me, really. Took the wedge from around my neck."

"That's fearsome. One o' them lone rogues, hey?" Wondering and sympathetic, Will shook his head. "Likely he'd a' slit your throat, sir, but didn't want to do no real sacrilege. Think he might still be here about?"

"No, no, I'm sure he was running away. Long gone by this time."

Will shook his head some more. "Well. You'd better liven up your limbs, sir, before you starts to climb down. I'm going on up, bit of a job to do for master."

"Job?"

"Aye." Will was already climbing again, seemingly meaning to go right on up into the spire.

Still on all fours, Derron peered down over the edge of the platform. Vincento's ginger-coloured hair marked a toy figure more than a hundred feet below. Down there the mysteriously moving cable ended in a dot, a ball of some kind that was tracing back and forth with sedate regularity. Derron had seen a pendulum of this size and shape before, somewhere. It had been used as a demonstration of . . .

Derron's muscles locked, after a moment in which he had been near falling over the platform's edge. He had suddenly realized what Vincento was looking at, what Vincento doubtless had been studying for most of the time Derron had been held captive. On old Earth they had honoured its earliest known inventor by naming it the Foucault pendulum.

"Honourable Vincento!"

Vincento looked around in surprise and annoyance to discover the young man, Alzay or Valzay or whatever his name was, hurrying toward him in obvious agitation, having evidently just descended from the tiny coiled stair where Will had begun his climb.

Valzay came hurrying up as if bringing the most vital news, though when he arrived all he had to relate was some imbecile story about a bandit. Valzay's eyes were looking sharply at the sawhorses and planks and the little wall of sand, even as he spouted pestiferous wordage that threatened to tangle Vincento's thoughts.

Vincento interrupted him. "Young man, I suggest you give your recital to the soldiers." Then he turned his back on the intruder. Now. If it was *not* the cable untwisting, and proved to be *not* some trick of the mountain above—then what? Certainly the bones of the cathedral were not creeping counterclockwise. But yet . . . his mind strained forward, sounding unknown depths . . .

"I see, Messire Vincento, that you have already discovered my little surprise." Derron saw very clearly how the game was certain to go, how it perhaps had gone already. But he also saw one desperate gamble that was still open to him, and he seized the chance.

"Your—little—surprise?" Vincento's voice became very deliberate. His brows knit as if presaging thunder, while he turned slowly back to face Derron. "Then it was you who sent that rascally friar to me in the night?"

The detail of the friar was confirmation, if any was needed, of what the berserker planned. "It was I who arranged—this!" Derron gestured with proprietary pride at the pendulum. "I must confess, sir, that I have really been here for several days; at first in the company of some friends, who aided me in this construction."

It was a big lie that Derron was improvising, and one that would not stand investigation. But if it had the initial impact that he hoped it would, Vincento would never want to investigate.

As he told the silent, grim old man how he and his imaginary aides had installed the pendulum, Derron visualized the berserker here at work, catlike, monkeylike, devilish, arranging mounting and cable and weight in order that:

". . . you see before you, Messire Vincento, a firm proof of the rotation of the globe!"

There was a start in the old eyes, but no real surprise. Beyond a doubt the desperate gamble had been justified. Now, to see if it could be won. Vincento had become a waiting statue, mouth twisted, eyes unblinking.

Derron spoke on: "Of course I have followed your example, distinguished sir, and that of several of our contemporaries, in protecting my rightful claim to this discovery while still keeping it secret for my own advantage in further research. To this end I have sent to several distinguished persons, in several parts of the world, anagram messages which encode a description of this experiment.

"Thus to keep the secret yet awhile was, as I say, my plan. But when word reached me of your present—difficulties—I found I could not stand idly by."

Vincento had not yet moved. "A proof of our globe's rotation, you say." The tone was flat, suspended.

"Ah, forgive me! I had not thought an explanation in detail would be—um. You see, the plane of the pendulum does not rotate, it is our globe that rotates beneath it." Derron hesitated briefly—it was just occurring to Valzay that old Vincento had most likely become just a little slow, a trifle senile. Derron put on what he hoped looked like a faintly indulgent smile, and spoke on, more slowly and distinctly. "At the poles of the world, such a device as this would trace daily a full circle of three hundred and sixty degrees. At the equator it would appear not to rotate at all." Speeding up gradually, he poured out in merciless detail his three and a half centuries' advantage in accumulated knowledge. "Between these extremes the rate of rotation is proportional to the latitude; here, it is about ten degrees per hour. And since we are in the northern hemisphere, the direction of apparent rotation is clockwise . . ."

From high above, Will was shouting down to his master; ". . . she be mounted free to turn any way, but there be nothing turning her!"

Vincento shouted up: "Come down!"

". . . bit more study if 'ee wants a sketch . . ."

"Come down!" The thick lips spat it out.

Derron kept the pressure on as best he could, switching the emphasis now to relentless generosity. ". . . my only wish of course being to help you, sir. I have put aside thoughts of personal advantage to come to your rescue. In bygone days you have accomplished very substantial things, and you must not now be cast aside. My lance is at your disposal; I will gladly repeat this demonstration of my discovery for the authorities in the Holy City, so that the entire world may witness——"

"Enough! I have no need of *help*!" Vincento made the last word an obscenity. "You will not—meddle—in—my—affairs. Not in the least degree!"

In his contempt and wrath the old man became a towering figure. Derron found himself physically retreating—even as he realized that he had won his gamble, that Vincento's pride was indeed as monumental as his genius.

The outburst of proud anger was short-lived. Derron ceased retreating and stood in silence as Vincento, shrinking once more under his burdens of age and weariness and fear, shot him a parting look of hate and turned away. Now Vincento would never use the Foucault proof, nor believe it, nor even investigate in that direction. He would force the whole thing from his mind if he could. The smallness and jealousy that were leading Vincent Vincento on to trial and humiliation existed not only in other men, but in himself.

Derron knew from history that at his trial Vincento would not only recant, he would go beyond what his judges asked or wanted of him, and offer to write a new pamphlet proving that the sun did after all fly in a circle around the world of men.

My only wish being to help you, sir. Vincento's shuffling figure dwindled at last to the end of the nave, and at last the door boomed shut behind him. Exhausted, Derron sagged against a column, hearing now in the silence the pendulum's unperturbed repeated hiss. Will came scrambling down the stair to scowl uncomprehendingly at him and then hurry on after his master.

And now even Vincento's tragedy could be forgotten for the moment. Real victory and real hope were powerful stimulants. They gave Derron energy enough to hurry out of the cathedral by a side door, and go skipping down a steep stair that led directly to the monastery. If the berserker had not also smashed the backup communicator hidden in his staff, he could transmit the joy of victory at once to all the Modern world.

The enemy had not bothered with anything in his cell. As he hurried toward it along the vaulted passage, an emergency summons from Operations began to throb in the bone behind his ear.

Brother Saile was puffing, though he had certainly been making no effort to hurry. The narrow cattle-path the friars were following went mostly up and down hill, winding its way through scrubby bushes and thin woods. Saile was actually hanging back, and with almost every puff of breath trying to discourage Brother Jovann's progress.

"I thought—to have said a few prayers in the village—would have been sufficient. These peasants as you know—are often foolish. They may have—greatly exaggerated—the depredations of this—supposed wolf."

"Then my own peasant foolishness is not likely to cause any harm," said Jovann, leading on implacably. They were miles from the cathedral now, deep in the wolf's supposed domain. Their peasant supplicants and guides had turned back through fear a quarter of a mile earlier.

"I spoke too harshly of them, may the Holy One forgive me." Saile wheezed to the top of a hill, and gathered breath for

161

readier speech on the descent. "Now if this one beast has really caused in a few days all the death and damage attributed to it, or even half so much, it would be utter folly for us to approach it unarmed as we are. It is not that I doubt for an instant the inscrutable wisdom of Providence that can cause a fish to leap for joy after you have released it, nor do I doubt the story that is told of the gentle little birds listening to your preaching. But a wolf, and especially such a wolf as this, is quite another..."

Brother Jovann did not appear to be listening very closely. He had paused briefly to follow with his eyes a train of scavenger-insects which crossed the path and vanished into the brush. Then he went on, more slowly, until a similar train appeared a little farther along the trail. There Brother Jovann turned aside and walked noisily into the brush, leading his companion toward the spot where it seemed the two lines of insects must intersect.

Staff in hand, Derron made the best cross-country time he could, running fifty steps and walking fifty.

"Odegard!" Time Ops had cried out. "There's another life-line just as vital as Vincento's right there with you. Or he was with you. Now he and one of the others have moved out a couple of miles, they're about to leave the safety zone. You've got to get there and protect him somehow. The berserker will have him cold if it's out there waiting!"

And of course it would be out there, in ambush or pursuit. The attack on Vincento had been in deadly earnest, as the first punch in any good one-two should be. But it was the second punch that was really expected to get through and do the damage. And humanity had been left wide open for this one.

Running fifty steps, walking fifty, Derron steadily covered ground along the bearing Operations had given him. He asked: "Just who am I looking for?"

And when they told him, he thought he should have guessed the name, should have been alerted by his first look into that loving face.

In the midst of the thicket there had been havoc. It had happened days ago, for the tree branches that had been broken were now quite dead. And though the insects were still busy amid the wreckage of bone and grey fur on the ground, there was no longer much for them to scavenge.

"This was a very big wolf," said Brother Jovann thoughtfully, bending to pick up a piece of jawbone. The bone had been shattered by some violent blow, but this fragment still contained teeth of impressive size.

"Very big, certainly," agreed Brother Saile, though he knew little about wolves. He had no wish to learn any more, and kept looking about him nervously. The sun was slanting into late afternoon, and to Saile the forest seemed ominously still.

Jovann was musing aloud. "Now what manner of creature can it be that deals thus with a big male wolf? Even as I in my greed have sometimes dealt with the bones of a little roast fowl . . . but no, these bones have not been gnawed for nourishment. Only broken, and broken again, as if by some creature more wantonly savage than any wolf."

The name of Brother Jovann symbolized gentleness and love to Modern historians as well as laymen, to sceptics as well as the orthodox temple-members who venerated him as a saint. Like Vincento, St. Jovan had become a towering folk-figure, only half-understood.

"We're just this hour catching on to Jovann's practical importance," said Time Op's voice in Derron's head as Derron ran. "With Vincento stabilized, and all our observers concentrated on the area you're in, we're getting a better look at it than ever before. Historically Jovann's lifeline goes on about fifteen years from your point, and all along the way it radiates support to other lines. What has been described as 'good-turn-a-day stuff'. Then these other lines tend to radiate life support in turn, and the process propagates on up through history. Our best judgement now is that the disarmament treaty three hundred years after Jovann's death will fall through, and an international nuclear war will wipe out our civilization in pre-Modern times if St. Jovann is terminated at your point."

When Time Ops paused, a girl's voice came in briskly: "A new report for Colonel Odegard."

Walking again, Derron asked: "Lisa?"

She hesitated for just an instant; then, business first. "Colonel, the lifeline that was described to you earlier as having an embryonic appearance is moving out of the safety zone after the other two. It seems to be travelling at a high rate of speed, faster than a man or a loadbeast can run. We can give no explanation of this. Also, you're to bear five degrees left."

"Understand." Derron bore five degrees left, as near as he could judge. He was getting out of the lowlands now, and there was a little less mud to impede his progress. "Lisa?"

"Derron, they let me come on because I said I'd tend strictly to business."

"Understand, you do that." He judged he had walked fifty steps and began to run once more, his breath immediately turning into gasps. "I just want to say—I wish—you were carrying my baby."

There was a small, completely feminine sound. But when Lisa's voice came back intelligibly it was all business again, with more bearing corrections to be given.

From the corner of his eye Brother Saile caught the distant movement of something running toward them through the trees and brush. He turned, squinting under the afternoon sun, and with surprise at his own relative calm he saw that their search for the wolf had come to an end. Wolf? The thing approaching should perhaps be called monster or demon instead, but he could not doubt it was the creature that had spread terror among the peasants, come now to find the men who dared to search for it.

Poisonous-looking as a silver wasp, the man-sized creature was still a hundred yards away, coming through the scrub forest at a silent, catlike, four-legged run. Brother Saile relized that he should now attempt to lay down his life for his friend, he should shove Brother Jovann back and rush forward himself to distract the thing. And something in Brother Sail wanted to achieve such heroism, but his belly and feet had no turned to lead, leaving him immobile as a statue. He tried a least to shout a warning, but even his throat was paralysed by fear. At last he did manage to seize Brother Jovann by the arm and point.

"Ah," said Jovann, coming out of a reverie and turning to look. A score of paces away the monster was slowing to a halt, crouching on its four slender legs, looking from one friar to the other as if to decide which of them it wanted. Peasants glimpsing the creature might call it wolf. Shreds of grey cloth festooned it here and there, as if it had been dressed and then had beast-like torn itself out of the garment. Naked and hairless and sexless, terrible and beautiful at once, it flowed like quicksilver as it took two rapid strides closer to the men. Then it settled again into a crouching, silent statue.

"In God's n-name come away!" Brother Saile whispered, through shivering jaws. "It is no natural beast. Come away, Brother Jovann!"

But Jovann only raised his hands and signed the horror with the wedge; he seemed to be blessing it rather than exorcising.

"Brother Wolf," he said lovingly, "you do indeed look unlike any beast that I have ever seen before, and I know not from what worldly parentage you may have sprung. But there is in you the spirit of life; therefore never forget that our Father above has created you, as He has created all other creatures, so we are all children of the one Father."

The wolf darted forward and stopped, stepped and stopped, inched and stopped again, in a fading oscillation. In its open mouth Saile thought he saw fangs not only long and sharp, but actually blurring with vicious motion like the teeth of some incredible saw. At last there came forth a sound, and Saile was reminded simultaneously of ringing swordblades and of human agony.

Jovann dropped to one knee, facing the crouching monster more on a level. He spread his arms as if willing an embrace. The thing bounded in a blur of speed toward him, then stopped as if a leash had caught it. It was still six or eight paces from the kneeling man. Again it uttered sound; Saile, halffainting, seemed to hear the creak of the torture rack and the cry of the victim rise together.

Jovann's voice had nothing to do with fear, but only blended sternness with its love.

"Brother Wolf, you have killed and pillaged like a wanton criminal, and for that you deserve punishment! But accept instead the forgiveness of all the men you have wronged. Come now, here is my hand. In the name of the Holy One, come to me, and pledge that from this day on you will live at peace with men. Come!"

Derron, approaching at a staggering, exhausted run, first heard a murmur of speech, and then saw the figure of Brother

Saile standing motionless, looking off to one side at something concealed from Derron by a thicket. Derron lurched to a halt, raising his staff but not yet aiming it. He knew now that Saile was not the berserker. What Operations had reported about the embryo-like lifeline had fitted in at last in Derron's mind with something the berserker had said to him in the cathedral, fitted in to make a wondrous kind of sense. Three steps sideways brought Derron to where he could see what Saile was gaping at.

He was only in time to see the berserker-wolf take the last hesitant step of its advance. To see it raise one metal paw—and with its steel claw-fingers gently touch the kneeling friar's extended hand.

"So, my guess was right, it had become a living thing," said Derron. His head was resting in Lisa's lap, and he could if he chose look up past her face at the buried park's real treetops and artificial sun. "And, as such, susceptible to St. Jovann's domination. To his love—I guess there's no other way to put it."

Lisa, stroking his forehead, raised her eyebrows questioningly.

Derron put on a defensive frown. "Oh, there are rational explanations. The most complex and compact machine the berserkers ever built, driven up through twenty thousand years of evolutionary gradient from their staging area—something like life was bound to happen to it. Or so we say now. And Jovann and some other men have had amazing power over living things—that's fairly well documented, even if we rationalists can't understand it."

"I looked up the story about St. Jovann and the wolf," said Lisa, still stroking. "It says that after he tamed it, the animal lived out its days like a pet dog in the village."

"That would refer to the original wolf . . . I guess the little change in history we had wasn't enough to change the legend. I suppose it was the berserker's plan all along to kill the original animal and take its place during the taming episode. Killing Jovann then might make people think he had been a fraud all his life. But tearing the original wolf into bits was an irrational, lifelike thing to do—if we'd known about that sooner we might have guessed what'd happened to our enemy.

166

There were other little clues along the way—things it did for no reason valid to a machine. And I really should have guessed in the cathedral, when it started babbling to me about passages between life and not-life. Anyway, Operations isn't as trusting as Jovann and his biographers. We've got the thing in a cage in present-time while the scientists try to decide what to . . ."

Derron had to pause there, to accommodate a young lady who was bending over him with the apparent intention of being kissed.

". . . did I mention how nice some of that country looked around there?" he resumed, a little later. "Of course the big hill is reserved for the rebuilding of the cathedral. But I thought you and I might drop into a Homestead Office sometime soon, you know, before the postwar rush starts, and put our names down for one of those other hilltops . . ."

And Derron had to pause again.

The Face in the Abyss

A remote valley hidden amid the towering peaks of the Andes and never before visited by civilised man is the scene of A. A. Merritt's classic novel of supernatural fantasy. The valley is inhabited by creatures long forgotten and races pledged to the resurrection of the glorious past.

Into this valley stumbles a young mining engineer, Nicholas Graydon. He defies the commands of the Snake-Mother's invisible but deadly servants and returns to the forbidden valley for the sake of Suarra, whom he loves. But Suarra can not be his until Graydon has persuaded the Snake-Mother to free the land of Yu-Atlanchi from Nimir, the Shadow of Evil. And the way to the Snake-Mother is beset with perils. Such as Lantlu, rider of dinosoaurs; the Lizard men. And, of course, the Dark Lord himself.